The GIRL
with the
DEEP BLUE
EYES

The GIRL
with the
DEEP BLUE
EYES

by **Lawrence Block**

A HARD CASE CRIME NOVEL

A HARD CASE CRIME BOOK
(HCC-121)
First Hard Case Crime edition: September 2015

Published by

Titan Books
A division of Titan Publishing Group Ltd
144 Southwark Street
London SE1 0UP

in collaboration with Winterfall LLC

ISBN 978-1-78329-750-4

Design direction by Max Phillips
www.maxphillips.net

Typeset by Swordsmith Productions

The name "Hard Case Crime" and the Hard Case Crime logo are trademarks of Winterfall LLC. Hard Case Crime books are selected and edited by Charles Ardai.

Printed in the United States of America

Visit us on the web at www.HardCaseCrime.com

This one's for my brown-eyed girl.

The GIRL
with the
DEEP BLUE
EYES

ONE

The phone woke him from a dream. At first his dream simply incorporated the sound in its narrative, and his dream-hand picked it up and his dream-voice said hello, and there his imagination quit on him, failing to invent a caller on the other end of the line. He said hello again, and the real-world phone went on ringing, and he shook off the dream and got the phone from the bedside table.

"Hello?"

"Doak Miller?"

"Right," he said. "Who's this?"

"Susie at the Sheriff's Office. Sorry, your voice sounded different."

"Thick with sleep."

"Oh, did I wake you? I'm sorry. Do you want to call us back?"

"No, it's what? Close to nine-thirty, time I was up. What can I do for you?"

"Um—"

"So long as it's not too complicated."

"On account of you're still not completely awake?"

He'd gotten a smile out of her, could hear it in her voice. He could picture her at her desk, twirling a strand of yellow hair around her finger, happy to let a phone conversation turn a little bit flirty.

"Oh, I'm awake," he said. "Just not at the absolute top of my game."

"Well, do you figure you're sharp enough for me to put you through to Sheriff Bill?"

"He won't be using a lot of big words, will he?"

"I'll warn him not to," she said. "You hold now, hear?"

Just the least bit flirty, because it was safe to flirt with him, wasn't it? He was old enough to be her father, old enough to be *retired*, for God's sake.

He let that thought go and went back for a look at his dream, but all that was left of it was the ringing telephone with no one on the other end of it. If the phone hadn't rung, he'd have awakened with no recollection of having dreamt. He knew he dreamed, knew everyone did, but he never remembered his dreams, or even that his sleep had been anything other than an uninterrupted void.

It was as if he led two lives, a sleeping life and a waking life, and it took the interruption of a phone call to make one life bleed through into the other.

"Doak?"

"Sheriff," he said. "How may I serve the good people of Gallatin County?"

"Now that's what I ask myself every hour of every day. You'll never believe the answer came back to me first thing this morning."

"Try me."

" 'Hire a hit man.' "

"So you thought of me."

"You know, there must be another fellow with your qualifications between Tampa and Panama City, but I wouldn't know how to get him on the phone. Susie said you were sleeping when she called, but you sound wide awake to me. You want to come by once you've had your breakfast?"

"Have y'all got coffee?"

"I'll tell her to make a fresh pot," Sheriff William Radburn said. "In your honor, sir."

＊

When he'd moved to the state three years ago, Doak had put up at first in a motel just across the Taylor County line. A Gujarati family owned it, and the office smelled not unpleasantly of curry. It took him a couple of months to tire of the noise of the other guests and the small-screen TV, and he let a housewife with a real estate license show him some houses. The one he liked was off by itself, with a dock on a creek that flowed into the gulf. You could hitch a boat to that dock, she'd pointed out. Or you could fish right off the dock.

He made an offer. When the owner accepted it, the agent delivered the good news in person. He'd had a beer going, and offered her one. She hesitated just long enough to signal that her acceptance was significant.

"Well," he said. "How are we going to celebrate?"

She gave him a look, and that was answer enough, but to underscore the look she twisted the wedding ring off her finger and dropped it in her purse. Then she looked at him again.

Her name was Barb—"Like a fishhook," she'd said—and while she wasn't the first woman he'd been to bed with since the move south, she was the first to join him in his room at the Gulf Mirage Motel. What better way, really, to celebrate his departure than by nailing the woman who'd facilitated it?

And she had a nice enough body, built more for comfort than for speed. Her breasts were nice, her ass was even nicer, and long before she'd shown him the house he wound up buying, he'd already decided not only that he wanted her but just how he intended to have her.

So when he went down on her he got a finger in her ass, and while she tensed up at first she wound up going with it. Her orgasm was a strong one, and had barely ended when he rolled her over and arranged her on her knees. He moistened himself in her pussy, and she was so warm and wet he had to force himself to leave, but he withdrew and she gave a little gasp at his departure and another when she felt him where his finger had been earlier.

She said, "Oh, I don't think—"

It wasn't much of a protest and he didn't pay any attention to it, forcing himself into her, feeling her resist, feeling her resistance subside, feeling her open for him only to tighten around him. He fucked her gently at first, then more savagely as passion took hold of him, and he cried out as he emptied himself into her.

He went away someplace for a moment, and the next thing he was aware of was lying on his back while she cleansed him with a washcloth. "Just a tame little thing now," she said, "but it like to split me in two a few minutes ago."

She took him in her mouth, and for an hour or so they found things to do. Then he got two more beers from the mini-fridge and they sat up in bed drinking them.

She said, "I hardly ever like that."

"Sex?"

"Silly. No, you know. Butt sex."

"You got into it pretty good there."

"I almost came. Which is something I never did."

"Came that way?"

"Never even enjoyed it, not really. I wonder if I ever could come that way."

"From getting fucked in the ass?"

"That sounds so *dirty*. Saying butt sex is bad enough."

"With an ass like yours—"

"I saw the way you looked at it. I knew what you wanted to do." She looked at him over the top of the beer can, weighed her words carefully. "I knew you wanted to fuck me in my ass."

"Your gorgeous ass."

"My gorgeous ass. My gorgeous ass which is a little sore, but I'm not complaining. I thought, oh, that's what he's gonna want to do, I just know it."

"And you hardly ever like it."

"And yet," she said, "I took my ring off, didn't I? Which reminds me." She got the ring from her purse, put it on her finger. "Now I'm married again," she said. "And I'm in desperate need of a shower. It's bad enough I'll be going home smelling of beer."

She showered, toweled dry. While she was dressing he went over and put his hands on her, but she said, "No, not now. And you can finish my beer for me, because I've had enough, and what I have to do now is stop at Cozy Cole's for my usual end-of-the-day glass of Chardonnay."

"So you can smell of wine instead of beer."

"Probably a little of both," she said, "with a top note of—no, never mind. Doak? We're not going to have a romance, are we?"

"No."

"No, we're not, which means we can probably do this every now and then without worrying that it'll blow up in our faces. But maybe I'm getting ahead of myself here. I mean, would you want to do this every now and then? Like maybe a couple of times a month?"

"I'd like that."

"Like friends with benefits, I guess they call it, except I don't even know that we'd be friends. Friendly, sure, but friends?"

"Just so we get the benefits."

"And I'd be interested in finding out if I can come that way."

TWO

It turned out she could. They established as much on her first visit to his new house, and it was a few days after that momentous occasion that he paid his first visit to the Gallatin County sheriff's office. It was a courtesy call, and a counterpart to one he'd made to the Taylor County sheriff not long after the state of Florida had licensed him as a private investigator. He didn't even know how much use he'd get out of the license, he could get by easily enough on his NYPD pension, but it never hurt to be on good terms with the local law, and he'd known retired cops back home with P. I. tickets who picked up the occasional piece of work through friends still on the job.

The sheriff of Taylor County turned out to be a piece of work himself, a slick article with a college diploma framed on his wall, and enough of a cracker accent to establish his bona fides as a good old boy. Doak could tell the man had an eye on the state house in Tallahassee, along with a snowball's chance of getting there, but he was young enough that it'd be another five years before he figured out that last part. Sheriff D. T. Newton was cordial enough, because he'd never be less than cordial to anyone without a reason, but Doak could tell right away they were never going to be Best Friends Forever.

The Gallatin County courtesy call was a good deal more fruitful. Bill Radburn was a genuine good old boy who didn't feel the need to act like one. If he'd ever had ambitions for higher office, he'd shed them somewhere along the way, and now all he wanted was to do his job well enough to keep the voters happy. His age was around sixty to Doak's forty-eight, and he liked ESPN and his wife's cooking, and the photo cube on his desk showed pictures of his grandchildren.

"Retired from the NYPD," he'd said. "Put in your twenty years?"

"Closer to twenty-five."

"And Tallahassee saw fit to give you a private license, though it's hard to guess what it'll do for you here in Gallatin County. Though I guess you never know, given the tendency folks have to get themselves in messes they can't get out of on their own."

"Oh, they do that down here, do they?"

"Now and again," the sheriff said.

And Doak had found occasion to drop in now and again himself, to drink a cup of coffee and swap war stories in a way he'd never have tried with D. T. Newton. Folks did get in messes, and now and then one of them turned up on his doorstep, and he got to pick up an honest fee for a little honest work. Sometimes he had to drive around, sometimes he had to talk to people, but a surprising amount of the time he got the job done and made the client happy without leaving his desk. More often than you'd guess, your computer could go around and knock on doors for you—and did it all without pissing off the person on the other side of the door.

None of his clients ever came to him through Bill Radburn. But then one day his phone rang, and half an hour later he was in the man's office on Citrus Boulevard. He'd said he'd done undercover work now and again, hadn't he? Well, here they were looking at a local fellow who very likely knew everybody with a badge within a fifty-mile radius, and he hated to call in the staties in Tallahassee if he didn't have to. So was he up for a little exercise in role-playing?

And the following afternoon he was sitting in his beat-up Monte Carlo in the parking lot of the Winn-Dixie, settling into

the role of a mobbed-up hit man from northern New Jersey—
"Bergen County, maybe you's heard of it"—agreeing to rid a
man with the second most profitable auto dealership in Gallatin
County of his business partner.

"He won't buy me out, he won't let me buy *him* out, and I
can't stand the sight of the son of a bitch," the man said. "So
what choice do I have here?"

"The man has a point," Radburn said, when they listened to
the recording of the conversation. They played it again for the
District Attorney, Pierce Weldon, whose vision of the future
was not limited to Gallatin County, and who clearly liked what
he was hearing.

"How's a man that stupid sell so many cars?" he wondered.
"Jesus, the dumb bastard lays it all out there in black and white,
or it will be when it's typed up. Though credit where it's due,
Mr. Doak."

"Just Doak," Radburn said. "Last name's Miller."

"My mistake, but all the same, Doak, I have to say you make
a very convincing hit man. I damn near bought your act myself.
I don't suppose you ever crossed the street to do a little moon-
lighting, did you?"

"If I did," he said, "I wouldn't say so. Be just my luck you'd
be wearing a wire."

They all assumed he'd have to testify, but the auto dealer's
attorney listened to the tape a couple of times and convinced
his client to plead guilty. After sentencing, Doak and Radburn
and Weldon shook hands all around. "And another solid citizen
wins himself a ticket to Raiford," the D.A. said. "That trophy
wife of his was all teary-eyed, but I don't guess she'll have too
much trouble finding somebody to elevate her spirits. Won't be
me, I know that much, and I'd like to think it's my high moral
principles but it may just be cowardice."

"They do dress alike," Radford said, "and it can be tricky to tell them apart."

"And it won't be you either, Grandfather William, because you're just too damned comfortable with your life as it is to reinvent yourself as Foxy Grandpa. But our cop-turned-hit man might find an opening here, so to speak. You're not married, are you, Doak?"

"Used to be."

"Was that a note of bitterness there? And you live alone? No entangling alliances? But maybe your sensitive self recoils at the idea of literally doing unto the wife what you've already done metaphorically to the husband."

"I did that once," he remembered.

"Oh?"

"Guy was a burglar, caught him before he could get the goods to a fence."

"And he had a hot wife?"

He nodded. "I knew better, but…"

"So many sad stories start with those four words."

"This wasn't that sad because it didn't last that long. She liked her booze, and after the third drink something in her eyes would change, and I realized I was afraid to fall asleep in her bed for fear that she'd stick a knife in me."

"Or go all Lorena Bobbitt on you."

"Jesus, there's a name from the past. Which is probably where it should stay."

And he knew he wouldn't hit on the auto dealer's wife, either. Because he was capable of learning from experience.

Besides, hell, she wasn't *that* hot.

THREE

The coffee Susie poured him was fresh, though not as strong as he'd have preferred. He settled in his chair across the desk from the sheriff and asked just who it was who wanted to dissolve a partnership.

"It's not like that this time," Radburn said, and stopped himself. "Except, come to think of it, it is."

"How's that?"

"Wife wants you to kill her husband," he said. "So it's a partnership, but of the domestic persuasion."

"And she wants me—"

"Well, not specifically, since she doesn't know you. At least I hope she doesn't, because that would be a deal breaker, wouldn't it? She's expecting a dead-eyed assassin, and who shows up but her buddy Doak from the Tuesday Night Bowling League."

"Wouldn't work."

"Her name's Lisa Otterbein, but her maiden name's Yarrow, and that's what she uses professionally. And I suspect she'll go back to it altogether once you kill George Otterbein for her."

"And we know she wants me to do this because—"

"Because three nights ago she sat down across a table from a fellow named Richard Lyle Gonson. Know him?"

"I don't think so."

"If you were looking to hire a hit man, he'd be a natural to sit across the table from. Not because you think he'd take the job, but because he'd probably know somebody who would. Or somebody who'd know somebody."

"He's not Reverend R. L. Gonson, the Congregationalist minister."

Radburn shook his head. "He's done, as the saying goes, a little of this and a little of that. He mostly gets away with it, but he's done a few bids, one of them federal. It's getting on for ten years since the last time he got out."

"He's behaving himself?"

"Does the bear give up a lifelong habit of sylvan defecation? Best he can do is learn to cover it up afterward. Even so, I had him for receiving last year, right around the end of hurricane season."

"But you couldn't make it stick?"

"He had something to trade."

"Ah."

"That's one way to cover up the pile in the woods. We got the chance to put away somebody who'd been giving us a lot more grief than Mr. Gonson ever did, and he saw the wisdom of having friends in law enforcement. So when Lisa let him know what she wanted, instead of telling her to go shit in her hat—"

"Or in the woods."

"—he said he knew the very man to call."

"And that man turned out to be you."

"It did. Neither of those names ring a bell? George Otterbein? Lisa Yarrow Otterbein?"

He shook his head.

"George's father started a restaurant-supply business. George inherited it and married money. Made a good thing of the business and invested some of the proceeds in local real estate. Rental properties, mostly, bringing in more money to go with the money he's already got."

"I'm guessing Lisa's a second wife."

"You New Yorkers, nothing gets past you. First wife was in one of those fifty-car chain pile-ups on 41. Foggy morning and one guy stops short and everybody hits him. Airbag deployed and Jo was unhurt, but somebody insisted she go to the hospital as a precaution, and while they were checking her they found something they didn't like, and so they checked some more, and she had cancer cells in everything but her hair."

"Jesus."

"Two months later she was gone. No symptoms before the accident, and it's hard not to think that if they hadn't found it she'd still be alive today. Which is ridiculous, but still."

Nothing to say to that. Doak sipped his coffee.

"You know the Cattle Baron? On Camp Road a mile or so north of Lee?"

"I've passed it. Never stopped."

"That'd be the best policy if you chanced to be a vegetarian. Just hold your breath and drive on by. Steak and seafood's what they've got on offer, and the steak's dry-aged prime Angus beef. After he buried Jo, George got in the habit of taking his dinners at the Baron. He was partial to their bone-in rib eye, which I can recommend, assuming you're not a vegetarian."

"I'll have to try it."

"You might want to wait a couple of weeks. All goes well, they'll have to find somebody new to show you to your table."

"Lisa's the hostess?"

"She showed George to his table every night, and I guess that wasn't all she showed him, and as soon as Jo was six months in the ground they went and got married. He'd had three children with Jo, two girls and a boy, and the oldest was the same age as Lisa. Now there's different ways kids will react to that sort of thing. Either the new wife's an angel for offering their daddy a second chance for happiness, or she's a gold-digging bitch. My experience, the more money's involved, the less likely she is to get the benefit of the doubt."

"Figures. She kept her job after they got married?"

Radburn shook his head. "Moved into his big house on Rumsey Road and set about being a woman of leisure. Spent some of George's money redecorating, bought some antiques in Tampa and some art in Miami. That held her interest for the better part of two years, and then she turned up one night back at the Cattle Baron, greeting her old customers by name and showing them to their tables like she'd never left."

"And the marriage?"

"I guess the honeymoon was over. If Lisa was working evenings, that had to cut into their together time. Far as anyone knew, they were comfortable enough with the new arrangement."

"Until a couple of nights ago."

"Until a couple of nights ago, when Rich Gonson and two other fellows came by to eat some meat and drink some whiskey. When Lisa brought the check to the table, she told him to stick around."

"And he did."

"Thought he was about to get lucky, according to him, but after his friends left and she sat down at his table, our girl was all business. 'Of course I don't know anybody in that line of work,' he told me—"

"Meaning he does."

"Wouldn't surprise me. What he told Lisa was he'd have to make a few phone calls, and the first call he made was to me. So last night I told Mary Beth she was about due for dinner out, and we had us a couple of shrimp cocktails and split the big rib eye, and I paid the tab myself instead of expensing it to Gallatin County."

"What a guy."

"Left a good tip, too. And took a picture when no one was paying attention." He found the photo on his iPhone, handed it across the desk. "Lisa Yarrow Otterbein."

"Very nice."

"She had long hair when she married George. I don't know when she got it cut, but it was short like that by the time she was back working at the Baron. I understand a woman's trying to tell you something when she cuts her hair, but they never gave me the code book. You ever seen her before? That you remember?"

He shook his head. "I'd remember," he said.

"Then she's probably never met you, either, so there's no reason she won't believe you're Frankie from New Jersey. Of course, the accent may give you away. You're starting to talk Southern."

"I am?"

"On the phone this morning. 'Have y'all got coffee?' That how they'd say it in Jersey?"

"Maybe South Jersey." He took another look at Lisa Otterbein's picture. Lisa Otterbein, Lisa Yarrow, whatever she called herself. The haircut, he decided, was probably a good idea, whatever the psychological motivation behind it. The short hair drew attention to her facial features, and it was a face you wanted to study. Beautiful, but that was almost beside the point.

"Give me your email, why don't you, and I'll send you the photo. Otherwise I get the feeling I'll never get my phone back."

FOUR

Back at his house, he set up a folding chair on the dock and sat there looking out through the mangroves. He hadn't bought a boat, hadn't even considered it, but one afternoon he'd stopped at a tackle shop and let the kid sell him enough basic gear so that he could bait a hook and drop a line in the water.

He'd tried that once, spent an hour or two on his dock, and whatever disappointment he'd felt in failing to haul in a fish was outweighed by his relief at not having to clean and cook his catch. The rod and reel were in his garage, along with the tackle box, and he'd never had the urge to repeat the experiment. But the dock was a nice place to hang out, as long as you didn't screw it up with a boat or a fishing rod.

He'd brought a magazine out onto the dock with him, but paid little attention to it. When he wasn't gazing off into the middle distance, letting his mind wander, he was looking at the photo the sheriff had sent him. Lisa, with her face framed by feather-cut dark hair.

A full-lipped mouth, but not overly so. Visible cheekbones, a pointy chin that just missed being sharp. Big eyes, accented with mascara, and what color were they, anyway? It was a good picture, but you couldn't tell the color of her eyes.

He could feel the fantasy, hovering out there on the edge of thought.

When had it first come to him? Maybe four, five years into his marriage. By then he'd already let go of his marriage vows, or at least the one about forsaking all others. He didn't go out chasing other women, but when the opportunity came along and the chemistry was right, he let it happen.

It wasn't the worst marriage in the world, but it never should have happened in the first place. He'd tried college and when that didn't work for him he went into the service. It was the peacetime army, and he'd finished his hitch and come home well before Operation Desert Storm and the Gulf War. A buddy was going to take the exam to get on the cops, so he went with him and passed, and went through the academy and came out with a gun and a badge and a stick.

And a uniform, in which he felt terribly self-conscious. But everybody did at first, and everybody got over it.

He met Doreen at a party. She had a cop for a brother, but nobody he knew. They started keeping company, and he was beginning to think it was time to break up with her when she told him she was pregnant. "Look, it's not the end of the world," she said. "I mean, we love each other, right? So we'd be getting married sooner or later anyway, wouldn't we?"

No, he thought, and no. He didn't love her and they wouldn't be getting married anyway. But what he said was, "Yeah, I guess you're right. When you look at it that way."

And it wasn't horrible. There were things he liked about being married. And he loved his son when he was born, and the daughter who followed a year and a half later.

Or did he? He figured he must, because you were supposed to.

So he cheated, when something came along, but he didn't chase, and it seemed to him that the cheating made it easier to stay married. Made life a little more interesting. The job was interesting, and the uniform no longer made him feel self-conscious, and anyway he was on track for a move into plainclothes. If the marriage wasn't interesting, well, the occasional vacation from it made it more tolerable.

The fantasy: *He meets this woman, and their eyes lock, and they connect in a way that neither of them has ever before connected with another human being.*

And that's just it, because they walk out of their separate lives and into a life together. Not a word to anybody, not a wasted moment to pack a bag or quit a job. They look at each other, and they connect, and they're in a car riding off together, or on a bus or a train or an airplane, and it's crazy and they know it's crazy but they don't care.

Of course it never happened. He met women, and now and then there was a connection, and sometimes it led as far as a bedroom, but it was never the magic mystical connection of the fantasy. Once or twice he thought he might be in love, and maybe he was, for a little while. And then he wasn't.

There was one woman—Cathy, her name was—and he imagined being married to her instead of Doreen. He could see her in that role, and he thought about it, and then one day he realized that he was able to envision her taking Doreen's place because she was in fact very like Doreen. And if the two of them wound up together, they'd just recreate the marriage he already had with Doreen. He'd be in the same place, and in short order he'd be cheating on Cathy, too, and the only difference would be the checks he'd be writing every month for alimony and child support.

There was no alimony in the fantasy, no child support either. That was because there was no past in the fantasy, no tin cans tied to the bumper of whatever vehicle whisked them away, him and his fantasy partner, into a wholly desirable if equally unimaginable future.

Well, that was fantasy for you.

Instead, he was stuck with the reality of a marriage that limped along. He was used to it, and he assumed Doreen was used to it, too, and then he went through a rough patch on the job, and that was working itself out, more or less, and Doreen surprised him by filing for divorce.

Nasty divorce, too. The boy was in college and the girl in her last year in high school, and they were young enough to think they had to take sides, and it was no contest, the side they took was their mother's.

Well, okay.

He could have retired when he had twenty years in, that was what a lot of guys did, but he'd always liked the job more than he'd disliked it, and your pension was better if you hung around for twenty-five. So he'd planned on doing that, and then Doreen did what she did, and all he wanted was to kiss everything goodbye.

It was like the fantasy, sort of, except there was nobody sharing it. Just his own middle-aged self and two mismatched suitcases, getting on a plane at JFK, getting off in Tampa. A night in a chain motel at the airport, then a cab to a used-car lot, where he'd paid cash for the Chevy Monte Carlo he was still driving. It would pass, as they said, everything but a gas station, but he led a low-mileage life and didn't mind what he spent on gas.

Then he'd pointed the car north. He'd been to Florida a few times over the years, mostly with Doreen. He wasn't sure where he wanted to be, but Tampa was too far south and the Panhandle was too far north, and when he got as far as Perry, in Taylor County, he thought it felt about right. He had dinner at Mindy's Barbecue and bedded down at the Ramada, and two nights later he moved to the Gulf Mirage to save a few bucks.

And so on.

A bird settled on a branch a few yards from him, then flew off. You could see a lot of birds from the dock, especially around sunrise and sunset. He couldn't tell one bird from another, but there were books, if he wanted to pursue the subject. And a pair of binoculars would make it easier to see what he was looking at.

And how long before the binoculars wound up in the garage, next to the fishing tackle?

He settled himself in his chair and let his eyes close, and the next thing he knew the phone was ringing.

"All set," Bill Radburn told him. "She'll come by the Winn-Dixie lot at half past eleven tomorrow morning. You'll be in a royal blue Chevy Monte Carlo parked all by itself at the rear of the lot. At least I think you will. You didn't cross me up by buying a new car, did you?"

"No, but it's closer to green than blue. I think it says 'teal' on the registration."

"Well, don't go run out now and get it painted. She'll be able to find you. I wondered about the Winn-Dixie, though. I had Susie check what made the papers the last time we did this, just to make sure they never mentioned where the sting went down. We're clear."

"Good."

"I guess. I checked with Motor Vehicles, and she'll probably be driving a silver-gray Lexus. But if she gets there before you, don't pull up next to her. Park off by yourself and let her come to you. I don't have to tell you why, do you?"

"So it's not entrapment?"

"That's the reasoning. Must have been worked out by some bright young fellow trained by the Jesuits. I'll tell you something, Doak. I know this isn't entrapment but I can't say it doesn't feel like it."

"She's the one who sat down with Gonson."

"Oh, she thought it up and brought it up, she's the one decided she'd rather be a real widow than a grass one. She's

trying to arrange a murder, and we prevent that murder by sup-
plying a fake killer for her to meet with. But if the whole point
is to keep a murder from happening, shit, all I'd have to do is
polish off another rib eye. When she comes over to the table,
what I do is put my cards on it. 'I know what you've got in
mind, sweetheart, and don't bother to deny it. And if anything
happens to your husband, I'll know just who to look at. So you
better either divorce him or pray he lives to be a hundred.' You
care to tell me that wouldn't work?"

"It probably would."

"Damn right it would. She'd miss out on a few years in an
orange jumpsuit and George would be spared knowing that his
wife wanted him dead. And I'd be shirking my duty."

"Which is to lock up the bad guys."

"And girls, right. And if she'll go so far as to hire a killer,
who's to say society is better off with her on the loose? I might
be able to frighten her out of having George Otterbein killed,
but would that scare some moral fiber into her?" A sigh. "So
we'll play this by the book. Eleven-thirty in the Winn-Dixie lot.
She'll be bringing a thousand dollars as earnest money, and it'd
be best if you could get her to hand it to you."

"Understood."

"And you won't forget to wear a wire, will you?"

"What an idea."

"And remember you're a Jersey boy. You wouldn't want to
slip and say something like, 'Bergen County, maybe y'all have
heard of it.' "

He watched the local news, the national news. Five minutes of
Pardon the Interruption on ESPN, five minutes of *Jeopardy*.
Took a shower, decided he could get by without a shave, then
changed his mind and shaved anyway.

Couldn't decide which shirt to wear. Crazy, he thought, and stupid in the bargain. He didn't have that many shirts, and nobody was going to notice what he was wearing, and it's not as though he was looking to make an impression.

Been a while since he'd had a good steak. No need to read more than that into it.

FIVE

And it was a good steak, no question about it, well-marbled and tender. The cliché about doughnuts notwithstanding, cops learned to eat well in New York, and at one time or another he'd had steak dinners at Keen's, Smith & Wollensky, and Peter Luger. If the Cattle Baron's rib eye wasn't the best he'd ever had, it was certainly in the top ten.

He ordered it black and blue, not sure if they'd know what that meant, and he wasn't reassured by the faint look of puzzlement on the face of the dishwater-blonde waitress. But she evidently passed the order on to a chef who knew what he had in mind, and his steak showed up charred on the outside and blood-rare within. It was a generous serving, accompanied by a baked potato and a side of creamed spinach, and it was almost enough to take his mind off Lisa Yarrow Otterbein.

Almost.

The fantasy, brought up to date:

He sits over a cup of coffee, watching her. She can't see him, but his gaze is strong enough for her to feel it, even though she doesn't know exactly what it is that she feels.

She approaches his table, asks him if everything is all right.

He says it is.

But none of their words matter. Their eyes have locked together, and something passes between them, a current as impossible to identify as it is to deny.

She says her name: "Lisa. Lisa Yarrow."

"Doak Miller."

"We close at eleven. That's when I get off."

"But we don't have to wait until then, do we?"

"No, of course not. I'm through here. As soon as you finish your coffee—"

He puts money on the table. "I'm done with my coffee," he says.

He gets to his feet. She takes his arm. They walk through the dining room and out of the restaurant.

She points to her car.

"We'll take mine," he says.

"Good," she says. "His money bought it. I don't want it anymore."

He holds the door for her, walks around the car, gets behind the wheel. The car starts up right away, and he pulls out of the lot and heads north on Camp Road.

They drive for twenty minutes in silence. Eventually she asks him where they are going.

"Do you care?"

She thinks about it. "No," she says at length. "No, not at all."

The reality:

She comes to his table without being summoned, or even stared at. She asks him if everything was all right. He says it was.

Their eyes never meet.

The blonde waitress brings the check. He takes a credit card from his wallet, thinks better of it, puts it back. And, as in the fantasy, puts bills on the table.

Back home, he booted up his computer, checked his email, dropped in at a couple of websites. Found something to Google, and let one thing lead to another.

Running it all through his mind.

He thought about—and Googled—Karla Faye Tucker. Killed some people with a pickax during a 1983 robbery in Texas, got herself convicted and sentenced to death the following year, and executed by lethal injection in 1999. She found God in prison, which is where He evidently spends a lot of free time, and the campaign for a commutation of her sentence made much of this conversion. She was an entirely different person now, her advocates stressed; kill her and you'd be killing someone other than the woman who'd committed the murders.

The other side pointed out that, even if the conversion was genuine, it had only come about because Karla Faye had a date with the needle. Yes, she'd earned herself a place in Heaven. No, she couldn't postpone the trip. Your bus is waitin', Karla Faye!

What brought the case to Doak's mind had nothing to do with arguments for and against capital punishment, an issue on which his views tended to shift anyway. But he remembered something someone had said right around the time that *60 Minutes* was airing the woman's story, and George W. Bush, still in the Governor's Mansion in Austin, was turning down her appeal:

"If she wasn't pretty, nobody'd give a damn."

Well, somebody would. The die-hard opponents of capital punishment would be on board no matter who she was or what she looked like. But if she'd had a face like a pizza, there'd have been fewer signatures on those petitions, fewer feet marching, and a lot less face time on network television.

But she was a pretty woman, maybe even beautiful. That got her more attention, got her special treatment.

So he was thinking about the woman he was going to meet tomorrow. Lisa Yarrow Otterbein, who was better looking than Karla Faye Tucker, and who, as far as he knew, had never even laid hands on a pickax.

The Wikipedia page showed a photo of Karla Faye Tucker, and he pulled up Lisa's photo on his phone and held it alongside of Karla Faye's for comparison.

No comparison, really.

Radburn's photo was a good one, he noted. Except that it was static, a single moment frozen in time, and she had one of those faces that kept changing, looking slightly different from every different angle, changing too as whatever was going through her mind played itself out on her face.

A man could spend a lifetime looking at a face like that.

Jesus, he thought.

He opened MS Word, clicked to open a new document. His fingers hovered over the keyboard, and then he changed his mind, just as he'd changed his mind about the credit card. He closed Word, then shut down his computer altogether.

Found a tablet. The old-fashioned kind, a yellow legal pad, ruled sheets of paper 8-1/2 by 11 inches. Uncapped a Bic ballpoint, began printing in block capitals.

He was at his desk for the better part of an hour. There were plenty of pauses, a lot of gazing off into the middle distance, chasing the thoughts that flitted across the surface of his consciousness. And from time to time he'd pick up his phone and find his way to her photograph.

A good photo, but there was so much it couldn't show. Including the color of her eyes.

They were blue.

He set the alarm for eight and woke at seven-thirty as if from a dream. But there were no dream memories, no clue to the dream's theme or subject.

He showered, dressed. He'd laid out clothes before he went to bed, and they were on the chair waiting for him—boxer shorts, dark trousers, a long-sleeved shirt with a tropical print. A parrot, a palm tree, just the sort of thing a snowbird would buy the day after he got off the plane.

He'd bought it himself in a strip mall halfway between Tampa and Perry. Hardly ever wore it since.

Along with the clothes, the chair held the recording device the sheriff had reminded him not to forget. He fastened the rig around his chest, clicked it on and off and on again, said "Testing, one two three," which was what everyone said under the circumstances, probably because it was easier than thinking of something else to say. He played it back, heard the words in his own voice.

It always surprised him, hearing his own voice. It was never the way he thought he sounded.

The shirt covered the wire. Nothing showed. He slipped his hand between two shirt buttons, switched the thing on, played the test again, then erased it. He said, "Recorded in the parking lot of the Winn-Dixie supermarket on Cable Boulevard in Belle Vista, Gallatin County, Florida, this sixteenth day of April in the year two thousand fourteen. Participants are J. W. Miller and Lisa Yarrow Otterbein."

Stopped it, played it back. He'd spoken in his everyday voice, but how much of that was New York and how much had turned Floridian was hard for him to tell. He'd speak differently as Frankie from Bergen County, and he wouldn't have to think about the accent. All he had to do was get the attitude right and the accent would follow.

He checked his wristwatch for the tenth or twentieth time. The time raced or crawled, it was hard to say which. He didn't want to do this, and at the same time he wanted to do it and be done with it.

＊

He circled the Winn-Dixie lot a few minutes before eleven, looked for a silver-gray Lexus, looked for any car parked off by itself.

Nothing. He drove a few blocks away and parked on the street. Checked the wire, made sure it was still working. Picked up the yellow pad, looked it over, shook his head at what he'd written.

Took out his phone, checked to see if anyone had called. He'd switched it from Ring to Vibrate before he left the house, because he didn't want to get a phone call while he was busy being Frankie from Jersey.

No calls.

He summoned up her photo. Surprising, really, that you couldn't determine the color of her eyes. They were such a vivid blue you'd think the camera couldn't help picking it up.

He put the phone away. Checked his watch again, and returned to the Winn-Dixie. The parking spot he picked was at the rear of the lot and over to the left. There were no other cars within thirty yards of it.

He was ten minutes early, which was about right. He should be here first. Let her come to him.

If she did.

He hadn't really entertained the possibility that she'd fail to show, but now it seemed highly probable. It was, after all, one thing to broach the subject to someone you knew, even as superficially as she knew Gonson. It was another thing to meet with a complete stranger and pay him a down payment on a contract killing.

She'd skip the meeting, he decided. She'd stay home and give it some more thought, and then she'd tell Richard Lyle Gonson that she'd changed her mind. Or she'd make up a story explaining why she'd been unable to get to the Winn-Dixie lot at the appointed hour, and looking to reschedule. And there'd be more phone calls all around, and tomorrow morning or the day after he'd be sitting where he was sitting now, only this time she'd show up, because she wouldn't pull the same crap twice. And—

And there she was. A silver sedan, but was it a Lexus? Cars tended to look alike these days—although nothing out there looked much like his Monte Carlo. But this was indeed a Lexus, he recognized the hood emblem, and it was skirting the several rows of cars huddled around the store entrance and heading instead for the rear of the lot.

She seemed to hesitate, settling at length on a spot one row in front of him and four spaces off to the left. She shut off the ignition, stayed behind the wheel.

Did she want a sign? All right, he could give her one. He flicked his headlights on and off, then on and off again. Was that entrapment? He decided it wasn't, not unless she was a moth.

Her door opened and she got out of the car. She was wearing a burnt orange top over a pair of powder-blue designer jeans. A tan leather bag rode her shoulder, and one hand pinned it to her side, as if to secure the thousand dollars.

He leaned across the passenger seat, opened the door for her. She hesitated for a beat, and he patted the seat in invitation. She got in and drew the door shut.

SIX

"Right on schedule," the sheriff said. "But I don't see the look of accomplishment that lit up your face the last time you wore a wire."

"No."

"I'd guess you got stood up, but you could have told me as much over the phone."

"No, she showed up," he said. "Simplest thing is to play it for you."

"Recorded in the parking lot of the Winn-Dixie supermarket on Cable Boulevard in Belle Vista, Gallatin County, Florida, this sixteenth day of April in the year two thousand fourteen. Participants are J. W. Miller and Lisa Yarrow Otterbein."

(beat)

"I don't know how to say this."

"Hey, take your time."

"Look, I made a big mistake. I was upset, I was angry, and I told…I don't want to say his name."

"I know who you mean."

"I never thought he'd take me seriously. I certainly didn't take it seriously myself, and when he got back to me and told me he'd made arrangements with you, I didn't know what to think."

"Maybe you need some time to think it over."

"No, all I need is for this whole incident to be as if it never happened. I'm not, not the sort of person who does this sort of thing."

"Whatever you say."

"*My God, I don't even kill bugs!*"

"*My wife's the same way. She makes me kill 'em for her. Which, when you stop an' think about it —*"

"*I take them outside and let them go.*"

"*Okay.*"

"*I told Mr....I told that man I never meant it, that it was a complete mistake, that he should get in touch with you and call it off. If you're sure, he said, then just don't show up. He'll get the idea. He doesn't even know your name, he's not going to turn up on your doorstep.*"

"*You coulda done that.*"

"*And maybe I should have, but I don't like loose ends. And why should you be stuck here waiting?*"

"*Very considerate.*"

"*This way it's all perfectly clear. I'm not at all interested in…what we talked about, and we can both go our separate ways and think no more about it.*"

"*Yeah, okay.*"

"*You've had to make a trip for nothing, and I apologize for that. If you feel you ought to be reimbursed for your time —*"

"*Hey, I got more time than I know what to do with. And it's very decent of you to show up on time and not leave me high and dry. But I get the feeling there's more to it than just tying off loose ends.*"

"*What do you mean?*"

"*Maybe there's a part of you wants to go through with it. I just now made a bet with myself, and you know what I bet? I bet you got an envelope in that purse and the envelope's got a thousand dollars in it. Do I win my bet?*"

(*beat*)

"*I thought there was a chance you would want to be reimbursed for your time and —*"

"And you were also giving yourself a chance to change your mind and go through with it."

"No."

"And you still got the option, you know. It's still your call. You want to call me off now, once and for all, fine. That's it and I'm gone. But if you want to change your mind back again, now's the time to do it."

"I don't—"

"Some bugs, you know, you can't just take 'em outside. They keep coming back until someone gets rid of 'em for you."

(sound of a car door opening)

"No, I'm not, I don't, no."

"Whatever you say."

"I was out of my mind with anger, and I poured a couple of drinks on top of the anger, and I said something crazy and even while I was saying it I knew I wasn't serious, I couldn't possibly be serious. I'm going now. This is over, okay? Because I really want this to be over."

(beat)

"Recorded at the Winn-Dixie lot, morning of April sixteenth, year is twenty-fourteen. Participants are J. W. Miller and Lisa Yarrow Otterbein. Over and out."

"'Over and out.' You were a lot more formal at the beginning."

He nodded. "By the time she got out of the car," he said, "what I said and how I said it didn't seem all that important. You and I are the only people who'll ever have to listen to it."

"Which is just as well, seeing as you came perilously close to entrapment toward the end there. All about those bugs that keep coming back inside, unless you let Frankie Boy hang a patch on your screen door."

"I know. But it was all slipping away. She was calling it off, and I figured I'd give her one last chance to call it back on again."

"I'm not blaming you. If she changed her mind once she could change it again, but once she's out of the car it's game over. Some of what she said was crap, you know."

"I had the feeling."

"I don't believe she had that second conversation with Rich, where she tries to get him to call it off and he says handle it yourself. He never mentioned any second conversation, never said a thing to indicate she was having second thoughts."

"Would he?"

"If the conversation ever happened, would he call and report it?" Radburn leaned back in his chair, folded his hands on his stomach. "Well, that's a question," he allowed. "Why would he bother? Still, she brought the thousand, didn't she?"

"She didn't show it to me."

"No, but she didn't deny it, either, and maybe it was in case you pitched a bitch about your time and expense, and maybe it was something else. You mind playing it again?"

They listened to the recording a second time through.

"What she's saying," Radburn said, "is convincing enough, but it's like her voice doesn't quite match the words. You know what I mean?"

"I think so."

"It's like she decided that this is gonna be her story, so that makes it the truth, so all she has to do is tell it. And she does tell it, and she never exactly sounds like she's lying—"

"But there's no feeling behind the words."

"There you go. Other hand, she's sitting next to a cool son of a bitch who kills people for a living. Some people might find that to be a case of inhibiting circumstances."

"It's easy for me to forget what a desperate character I am."

"If I had to guess, Doak, she meant it when she sat down with Gonson. She was working the floor that night, so she couldn't have been all that drunk. A drink or two, maybe, and maybe she'd had a fight with George before she left the house and was still pissed at him. But when she brought up the subject, she genuinely wanted him dead."

"And then she got to thinking it over."

"Same as anybody would do. That's a pretty big step, paying to have a man killed, even if you happen to be married to the fellow. And once you do it, there's no Undo button."

"No."

"Easier to hit that button before there's anything needs to be undone. Pull the plug, abort the mission." He made a tent of his fingertips. "And when it's time for the meeting, just stay home."

"But she didn't."

"No, she showed up, and she brought along the thousand dollars, because you never know when you'll see just the perfect little black dress." He peered at Doak. "I dunno," he said. "Maybe you're the problem."

"Me?"

"Say she got in the car, all set to go for the deal, and she took one look at your ugly face and said, 'Hell no, I don't want this degenerate getting anywhere near my George.'"

"That must be it. How big a payday was this degenerate supposed to be getting?"

"You mean how much is Gallatin County going to pay you? I hadn't even thought about that, but—"

He was shaking his head. "No, don't worry about that. I spent a few minutes sitting in my car, and I had better-looking company than I generally get. This can be my gift to the county. No, what I'm wondering is what Frank the Exterminator was supposed to get for his professional services."

"Haven't we been saying it all along? A thousand dollars in front."

"In front of what?"

"Oh," Radburn said.

"Because even in South Jersey, even in fucking Camden, you can't expect to hire a hit man for a total price of a thousand dollars."

"No, of course not. That was just a down payment."

"Not even that, really. Earnest money, to show good faith. Before the deal went down, she'd be expected to come up with half the fee."

"Sounds reasonable."

"Traditional, anyway. But half of what, Bill? Did anybody set a price?"

Radburn frowned, thinking about it. "As far as I can remember, the only number I ever heard was one thousand."

"She couldn't have thought that was all she was going to have to pay. Didn't your friend Gonson quote her a price?"

"He wouldn't, not without letting me know about it. What he most likely did is told her the man she met with would discuss terms with her. Which you never had to do, on account of her pulling the plug."

"Right."

"Something the matter?"

"I don't know. It never occurred to me I was going to have to negotiate a price. I wasn't prepared, I wouldn't have known how much to ask for."

"You'd have come up with a number."

"Well, I guess. If I had to."

"Suppose you had to come up with one now. What would you say?"

"Jesus, I don't know. Fifty?"

"Fifty thousand?"

"Why, is that too low? Too high? What?"

"No, it sounds about right. This isn't New York or L.A., after all. It's not even Miami or Atlanta. But, uh, Doak? She called the whole thing off, and even if she didn't there was never going to be any cash changing hands beyond that thousand dollars we've been talking about. So what terrestrial difference could it make what price she might have thought she'd be paying?"

"Well, I can't really say," he said. "Not when you put it that way. But it sort of seems I ought to have some idea how much money I just missed out on."

SEVEN

It was a few minutes past two when he shook hands with the sheriff and got out of there. About the time he'd pushed the Play button and started the tape, there was a crack of thunder and the skies opened up. It had come down heavy and hard for twenty minutes, just enough to take the edge off the heat, but now the sun was hotter than ever, and what was left of the rain was rising as steam from the pavement.

He walked halfway to his car, then remembered he hadn't eaten anything since he left the Cattle Baron the night before. No breakfast, because he hadn't felt like putting food in his stomach with the meeting at the Winn-Dixie coming up. And nothing after she got out of his car, leaving him to watch her drive off in her Lexus.

There was a diner around the corner from the county offices, and the lunch crowd had thinned down by now. He took a booth in back and studied the mile-long menu, which essentially included every dish the chef/proprietor had ever heard of. The place was called Mykonos, although the original Greek owner had long since sold out to a Chinese couple from Havana. They still had some Greek dishes on the menu, and he'd had the spanakopita once, and it wasn't bad.

This time he had a cheddar omelet and fries and drank two cups of coffee. Someone had left a copy of *USA Today* on the next table, and he turned the pages while he ate, but nothing much registered. He was on his second cup of coffee when he remembered to check his phone. It was still on Vibrate, and in his right front pants pocket, with his wallet between it and his thigh. If it ever vibrated, he never felt it.

There'd been a single call at 1:14, there was a seven-word message on his voicemail. "It's Barb, call me when you can."

He had his thumb poised to place the call, then stopped himself. No, not just yet.

The Monte Carlo was like an oven. He'd meant to leave a window open, but it was just as well he hadn't, considering the way it had poured. Now, though, he was paying for it. The car had factory air, it would be hard to find a car anywhere in the state that didn't, but the years had taken their toll on it. Well, he thought, that was true of everything in the car, including its driver.

Especially its driver.

He drove home, got out of his clothes and under the shower. Afterward he put on a robe and cracked a beer. He thought about Barb Hamill, and what she liked to do, and weighed the pros and cons of having her come over. The beer was about half gone when he picked up the phone and made the call.

It went directly to voicemail. "Doak," he said, "returning your call," and rung off.

By the time she called back, the beer can was empty and he was stretched out on the couch, dozing off while an old movie played on his TV.

"I knew it was you," he said.

"The miracle of Caller ID."

"No, before I looked. See, I was taking a nap, and I woke up good to go."

"You mean the little corporal was standing at attention? And that's on account of it was me on the other end of the phone? Honey, I'm flattered, but knowing you it could've been anybody with a pussy."

"Now that's not true."

"Or even a tranny," she said, "if God had blessed her with a nice ass and a good boob job. Speaking of which, did you ever?"

"Did I ever what? Oh, have a tranny? Christ, no."

"Why not? I mean, out of curiosity if nothing else. What do they call them? Chicks with dicks? There's one or two advertise on Craigslist, and I saw a picture one time, and I have to say she had all the ingredients."

"And then some."

"You know I've never been with a woman, and these days that's something I almost feel I have to apologize for, like it's this embarrassing virginity I never got around to losing. But a pre-op tranny might be the best of both worlds."

"Oh?"

"I could cuddle up to her tits and play with 'em, which would be fun, but one thing about being with a woman is she would probably expect me to eat her pussy, and I'm not sure I'd want to do that, you know? But a tranny wouldn't have a pussy, not if she was pre-op. She'd have a dick, and you know how I feel about dicks."

"I remember."

"Of course I couldn't expect her to have a dick as nice as yours, but a dick's a dick, you know? I could suck it while I played with her tits, and maybe if I asked real nice I could get her to fuck me with it. What do you think?"

"I think you should put that perfect ass of yours in your car," he said, "and bring it over here."

"Oh, Doak, baby, I wish. That's what I had in mind when I called, not all this tranny stuff but your dick and some things we could do with it, places we could put it. But that was then, when I had a few unbooked hours staring me in the face, and now I've got appointments stacked up clear to dinner. And I'd love to cancel one of them, fuck, I'd love to cancel *all* of them, but I can't, I flat can't."

"Oh."

"I got you hot and bothered, didn't I? Talking like that."

"What gives you that impression?"

"Well, you're not the only one. I'm all wet. I'm in my office, I've got the door closed, I've got half an hour before I have to be anywhere. Hold on a sec, I want to take off my panties. There, that's better, now I can touch myself. Oh, God, I'm soaking wet."

"I can imagine."

"Can you? Are you touching yourself, honey?"

"Yes."

"You want to take a moment to get a Kleenex? Or a hankie? Of course you wouldn't need anything if I was there because I've got a mouth and an ass and a pussy and you could choose which one you wanted to come in. Oh, Jesus, I've got my finger in my ass and my thumb on my clit, and it kills me that I have to waste one hand on the fucking cell phone, but if I put the phone on speaker the whole office could hear us. Is this good, honey? Is it working?"

"It's working."

"You know what we could do? You and me, we could tag-team that tranny. She's just the cutest thing, Doak, blonde hair and perfect skin with an all-over tan, and tits so perfect you'd swear she grew them all by herself, and a gorgeous ass, and you can fuck her in the ass while I suck her cock, oh, and now you're both fucking me, I'm riding her cock while you're in my ass, and we're both fooling with her tits, oh, Jesus…"

"Oh my," Barb said. "Well, that's a first. That's something we never did before."

"You're full of surprises."

"Well, I guess. I keep surprising myself. I came really hard. I hope I didn't make a lot of noise."

"You were a perfect lady."

"I did all the talking, didn't I? You barely got a word in edgewise. But it was having you there that made it so exciting. I hope you had that Kleenex."

"Well."

"Or was it a hankie?"

It was neither, because fairly early on he'd stopped touching himself, and his own excitement had ebbed even as hers had heightened. He'd remained an avid spectator, caught up in her rich fantasy, but the urge to complete the act subsided, and his erection along with it.

"I don't even know that I'd want to do all that," she said now. "Or any of it, even. You ever done any kind of threesies?"

"Not lately."

"But in the past? Two gals and a guy, would be my guess."

"Every man's fantasy," he said, "and when it finally came along it was more awkward than anything else."

"Oh, now that's disappointing to hear. The best thing about fantasies is they're always perfect. Nobody has bad breath, nobody has trouble getting it up. And every orgasm is perfect. Well, mine was pretty great just now."

"I'm not complaining."

"And yet," she said, "there's a kind of lingering horniness after coming that way. Like I didn't actually *do* anything, and I kind of want to."

"But you've got appointments."

"Oh, I do, and then it's home and hearth for the duration. Which means hubby's in line to get one amazing blow job before the day is done."

"And he'll never know what inspired it."

"What he'll also never know," she said, "is that all the while I'll be picturing him with an amazing set of tits. And I'll have a finger in his butt, which we've recently established that he kind of likes, but the man hasn't got a clue where Mama learned *that* little trick. Oh, look at the time. I've got to get off."

"I thought you already did."

"Oh, funny. Verrry funny."

EIGHT

From six to seven he watched half an hour each of local and national news, then put on the baseball game. The Rays were hosting the Blue Jays at Tropicana Field, and he watched the Toronto pitcher retire the first twelve batters he faced, striking out eight of them.

He wanted to get something to eat, but was reluctant to leave the house until some killjoy broke up the kid's no-hitter. There was some cereal left, some pretentious granola that promised you'd be saving the planet if you ate enough of it, and the milk smelled fresh, or at least it didn't smell sour. He ate in front of the TV, and in the sixth inning the pitcher walked the Rays' first baseman, so that was the end of his perfect game, but the next man up hit into a double play, so he still had a shot at facing only twenty-seven batters, which the announcer kept calling a numerically perfect game.

In the top of the eighth the kid had a three-run cushion, and his fast ball was still getting over at upwards of ninety-two miles an hour. He struck out the first batter, got the second on an easy grounder to the shortstop, took the third to three-and-two before he got him to pop up. Except it was more of a blooper, hit off the end of the bat, just out of reach of both the shortstop and the center fielder, and the game was suddenly no longer perfect numerically or otherwise, and no longer a no-hitter.

The next batter walked, and the one after doubled off the wall in right, and now it was no longer a shutout. And the kid suddenly couldn't find the plate, and walked the next Blue Jay on four pitches. The pitching coach came out to steady him, and let him face one more batter, which turned out to be a mistake when the batter in question hit one out. That made the score 5–3, and that was enough for the manager. It was also enough for Doak, who turned off the set.

He got dressed, got in his car. The night was cool enough to roll down the windows and get along without the A/C. He drove, put the radio on, turned it off.

Thought about the phone call. Phone sex, he guessed, was the term for it. Thought not about the call's content but about his own response to it.

The tranny was beside the point. He didn't think that was something he needed to try in real life, but it had been acceptable enough on a fantasy level. Barb had made it all exciting, and it hadn't ceased to be exciting, but he had somehow stopped being excited.

What he realized now was that had been his choice. He'd made an unconscious decision not to continue, when to do so would lead to a climax. He'd decided that wasn't what he wanted, and he'd instructed his body accordingly. He'd gone on listening, and he'd gotten a decent amount of secondhand satisfaction out of Barb's very audible orgasm, but for him the war was over.

All that remained was to lie about it. Though he hadn't quite lied, had he? *I'm not complaining,* he'd told her, and he hadn't been, so where was the falsehood in that?

Interesting, his choice.

Saving it, was he?

Maybe, but that was taking a lot for granted, wasn't it? He was taking a long drive on a dark night, along roads he didn't know, toward a place he'd never been. That was true, he realized, in a literal sense, and perhaps it was figuratively true as well, because he hadn't been down this road before, and there was no way to know what was at the end of it.

Well, one way. The same way you found out what the future held, and you didn't need a crystal ball for it, either. All you had to do was wait and see what happened.

The place he was looking for was on Florida 129 a mile and a half south of Live Oak, and when a sign welcomed him to that town he knew he'd overshot. He got the car turned around and backtracked, and there it was on the right, a fair amount of neon, a sign that said Kimberley's Kove, a one-story concrete block structure with its windows mostly blacked out, and seventeen vehicles, most of them pickups, clustered on the asphalt.

The Monte Carlo made eighteen, and he knew the number because he took the time to count them. Eleven pickups, two motorcycles, and five sedans including his own, which didn't stand out from the others. They were all of its vintage, and they too looked as though they'd been driven hard on bad roads.

He could call it a night and go home. It wouldn't take any longer than it had taken to get here, and it would go quicker, because any route always seemed longer the first time you drove it.

He checked his watch, found out it had taken him less time than he'd figured, even with missing the place on the first pass. So leaving now would be a bit previous, as he'd heard people say.

And all that driving had raised a thirst.

Inside, there was a long bar on the left, a juke box as big as any he'd ever seen, an unattended dance floor, and a dozen or so dark wooden tables on the right, with more tables in the rear. There were a few more customers than he'd seen vehicles, but not many, and none of them paid him any real attention. A few heads turned when he walked in, noted his arrival, and turned away.

The juke box was playing an oldie, Waylon Jennings singing

about how he was crowding forty and still wearing jeans. Which summed up the crowd, as far as that went. They all looked to be over thirty and no more than fifty, and the majority of them were wearing denim, including all five of the women.

He didn't see a waitress, but did see another patron get a pair of longneck bottles from the bar and carry them back to a table. Doak went to the bar and asked for Pabst. That's what the fellow had been carrying, Pabst Blue Ribbon, and that would do, as he didn't really care what he drank.

He paid for the bottle, carried it to an empty table. Crowding fifty, he thought, but instead of jeans he was wearing the same dark slacks he'd worn to the Winn-Dixie. Different shirt, though. Short sleeves, and sort of a windowpane check.

Christ, was it still the same day?

He nursed the beer, taking small sips from the bottle. He looked over at the door when it opened, and a woman with unconvincing red hair took two steps inside and asked the room if Whitney had been around. Somebody told her he hadn't. "Well, shit!" she cried, and stormed out, leaving the door to slam behind her.

Another five minutes, maybe ten, and the door swung open again. Heads turned, but no one spoke to the new arrival.

She was wearing jeans, and if she wasn't yet crowding forty she was gaining on it. She stood for a moment, letting her eyes adjust to the dim lighting, and then she found him and walked without hesitation to his table.

She sat down, and they looked at each other. She said, "Now what?"

Jesus, the blue of her eyes.

NINE

What really happened in the parking lot of the Winn-Dixie:

Her door opened and she got out of the car. She was wearing a burnt orange top over a pair of powder-blue designer jeans. A tan leather bag rode her shoulder, and one hand pinned it to her side, as if to secure the thousand dollars.

He leaned across the passenger seat, opened the door for her. She hesitated for a beat, and he patted the seat in invitation. She got in and drew the door shut.

Before she could say anything, he held up his left hand like a stop sign, put his right index finger to his lips. She froze, and her eyes widened.

He opened the top two buttons of his shirt, moved the fabric to reveal the rig he was wearing. It wasn't recording, but she didn't know that, so he made a show of uncoupling a connection and holding the two ends an inch apart.

Once again, he held his finger to his lips. He picked up the yellow legal pad, the top sheet covered in his deliberate block printing. She glanced at the pad, then at him. He shook his head, pointed again at the pad, indicating that she should read it.

The first page was an explanation. It had taken him several drafts to get it right, laying it all out, telling her that her friend Gonson had gone straight to the sheriff, that he'd been hired to get her to incriminate herself and capture the evidence on a recording. A denial wouldn't help her right now, and the best course of action for her was not to say a word.

NOD IF YOU UNDERSTAND.

She raised her eyes to his, then returned them to the yellow pad. And nodded.

THE NEXT PAGES ARE A SCRIPT. IT'S THE CONVERSATION YOU AND I ARE GOING TO HAVE. READ IT ALL THE WAY THROUGH SILENTLY. DO THAT THREE TIMES.

She looked at him, puzzled. He nodded, and she thought a moment, and answered his nod with her own.

After the silent reading, a single rehearsal. He had his own copy of the script, and they sat side by side, he behind the wheel, she in the passenger seat, and read their lines in turn. He stopped her once to correct her emphasis on one line, but otherwise he let her go straight through it.

A little stiff overall, he thought, but maybe stiff was okay. It was better for her to be slightly wooden rather than overly and unconvincingly expressive.

Another run-through wouldn't hurt a bit, but it would take time, and they didn't have it to spare. Time to go with what they had.

He clipped the rig together again, pressed Play:

"Recorded in the parking lot of the Winn-Dixie supermarket on Cable Boulevard in Belle Vista, Gallatin County, Florida, this sixteenth day of April in the year two thousand fourteen. Participants are J. W. Miller and Lisa Yarrow Otterbein."

He hit Pause. They looked at each other, and he hit Record and cued her. She took a breath, steeled herself, and went for it.

"I don't know how to say this."

"Hey, take your time."

"Look, I made a big mistake. I was upset, I was angry, and I told…I don't want to say his name."

"I know who you mean."

"I never thought he'd take me seriously. I certainly didn't

*take it seriously myself, and when he got back to me and told me
he'd made arrangements with you, I didn't know what to think."*

All the way through to the end of it. Turning pages carefully,
trying to avoid a rustling sound that the wire might pick up.

All the way through to:

*"Some bugs, you know, you can't just take 'em outside. They
keep coming back until someone gets rid of 'em for you."*

(sound of a car door opening)

"No, I'm not, I don't, no."

"Whatever you say."

*"I was out of my mind with anger, and I poured a couple of
drinks on top of the anger, and I said something crazy and even
while I was saying it I knew I wasn't serious, I couldn't possibly
be serious. I'm going now. This is over, okay? Because I really
want this to be over."*

He stopped the tape, nodded to indicate his satisfaction with her
performance. Then he switched it on again to record his wrap-up:

*"Recorded at the Winn-Dixie lot, morning of April sixteenth,
year is twenty-fourteen. Participants are J. W. Miller and Lisa
Yarrow Otterbein. Over and out."*

Then one last page for her to read over in silence, explaining
that this would cover her, but that she could never again try to
find anybody to kill her husband or anybody else, that the two
of them could never be seen together in public, that they could
never talk on the phone or communicate by text or email, that
all of those forms of communication left an ineradicable trail
that could put them both behind bars.

When she finished he took the pad from her, printed rapidly
in the usual block caps:

I NEED TO SEE YOU TONIGHT. WHEN DO YOU GET
OFF WORK?

She took the pen, wrote: I COULD CALL IN SICK.

He shook his head. AFTER WORK IS BETTER.

11:15. TOO LATE?

11:15 OK. WHERE? GOT TO BE WHERE NOBODY EITHER OF US KNOWS WILL SHOW UP, NOT IN OR NEAR GALLATIN COUNTY.

She had to give it some thought.

SOMEPLACE YOU KNOW BUT NEVER GO TO, he added.

And then she came up with Kimberley's Kove, and wrote down the name and location and how to get there.

MIDNIGIIT?

MIDNIGHT.

Midnight would work. Midnight was fine.

TEN

He asked her what she'd like from the bar. She looked at his Pabst longneck, shook her head. "Not beer," she said. "And this is no place to get fancy. You wouldn't want to ask them to make you a mixed drink."

" 'Shucks, ma'am, we's just plain country folks here.' "

"I wonder what the wine's like."

"Red or white?"

"That'd be the two choices. Oh, white, I guess."

He went to the bar and came back with four ounces of white wine in a small water tumbler. She raised the glass and he touched it with his beer bottle.

"Well, it could be worse," she said, after a small sip. "Although it doesn't taste much like wine."

She offered him the glass. He noted the trace of her lipstick on the rim, and allowed himself to drink from the same spot.

"I see what you mean," he said. "Maybe it's not."

"What else could it be?"

"Sour grape juice, watered down some and spiked with grain alcohol."

"People do that? Why would anyone—"

"Same reason they'd make any kind of bootleg," he said. "It's cheaper."

"You'd think jug wine would be cheap enough." She took another experimental sip, then said, "Oh, and consider yourself kissed."

"Huh?"

"We both drank from the same spot on the same glass. 'Consider yourself kissed' is what you say when that happens. You never heard that before?"

"No."

"I guess we know different things. You know how to make bad wine and I know what passed for sophisticated wit at Foxcroft."

"Is that where you went to school?"

"Not exactly. Jacob Tendler High, on Goodrich two blocks off Hennepin."

"Hennepin."

"That ring a bell?"

"It's a main drag somewhere, isn't it? Minnesota?"

"Minneapolis. What did you do, read it somewhere?"

"Read it or heard it on the news, and evidently it got stuck in my mind. That's where you're from? Minneapolis?"

"A few different places, and Minneapolis was one of them. My mother kept hooking up with men who felt a need to relocate. Then they'd do it again, only this time they wouldn't tell her, and she'd have to go and hook up with somebody else, some other shifty-eyed loser with an urge for going. I got the same urge myself one day, hopped on a bus and left the driving to Greyhound."

"And the Foxcroft lingo?"

"Lingo," she said. "I like that. At Foxcroft we'd say *patois*. Or maybe we wouldn't, maybe I'm misusing the word. 'Consider yourself kissed.' I read it in a book, and it stuck in my mind the way Hennepin did in yours. Don't ask me which book because I read so many of them, all about these preppy girls. Oh, isn't that Emmy Lou? What's the matter?"

"I thought there wouldn't be anybody here that you know."

"Well, I know her, but she wouldn't know me from Eve. On the jukebox, Emmy Lou Harris."

"Oh."

She lifted her glass, set it down untasted. "I've never been here before," she said, "and I don't know any of these people except the ones on the jukebox, and I can't say I want to. I picked this place because I remembered seeing it from the road and thinking how perfectly lowdown it looked, but aside from that I don't know anything more about it than I do about Foxcroft or Miss Porter's. I don't even know your name."

"It's Doak."

"And mine's Lisa, but you know that. You know a whole lot more about me than I know about you."

"I guess I do. But there's a lot I don't know."

"All I know about you is you like your rib eye cooked black and blue. That was a new one on Cindy, and she was impressed."

"Cindy? Oh, the blonde."

"I guess you must have been in the mood for a steak, but that's not why you came, is it? You wanted a look at me."

"I did."

"Oh, there's another old friend of mine. His name's Waylon."

He nodded. "Somebody played the song earlier, right after I got here."

"I like that the jukebox is all oldies. I don't think they planned it that way. I think they just can't be bothered to buy any new records. Can I ask you something?"

"Sure."

"Who the hell are you? Some kind of a cop, but what kind? And why would you wait for me to take the bait and then let me off the hook?"

He was considering his response when she added, "Or maybe I'm not off the hook yet."

"I don't really know much about fishing," he said. "The house I bought has a dock you could hitch a boat to, except that I don't own a boat and don't want one. But you can just fish right off the dock, and I bought a rod and reel, your basic beginner's outfit, and I gave it a try, and it didn't take me long to figure out it wasn't likely to turn into a lifelong passion."

"You never went fishing before?"

"Years ago, with a friend who kept a boat at City Island. Four of us out on the water for three hours, drinking beer and eating pizza, and nobody caught a thing."

"I don't know where that is."

"City Island? It's up in the Bronx."

"New York."

"That's right."

"That's what I thought in the car, from the accent. But it was stronger then."

"Part of the act."

"Oh."

"The sheriff says my accent's slipping, that I'm starting to sound Southern. I don't know if he's right."

"Florida, this part of it, is all different accents. You've got people in Belle Vista who moved here from all over the country, and you've got others who're still living on roads that were named for their great-grandfathers."

"That'd be me, if my grandpa's name was Osprey."

"That's where you live? Osprey Drive? I know where that is."

"So do I, but then I'd have to or I'd never find my way home. Is your accent Minnesota? There was that movie, *Fargo*, but you don't sound like that."

"We moved too much for me to have an accent. Or if I do, it's just a blend. Standard American, I think they call it. Doak."

"What?"

"I don't know. I was just saying your name. We've got to talk and we can't, can we?"

"I thought that's what we were doing."

"No, there's a conversation we need to have and we're just dancing around it. When I first noticed this place, Kimberley's Kove, and the tattooed dude behind the bar can't be Kimberley, can he?"

"Probably not."

"Maybe Kimberley got sent home because she failed her spelling exam. K-O-V-E is just so fucking K-Y-O-O-T, you know?"

"When you first noticed the place…"

"Right. I also noticed, maybe half a mile south of here, a place called Tourist Court. Oddly enough, they spelled Court with a C."

"On the left," he remembered.

"A twelve-unit strip motel, plus four cabins. It's about what you'd expect for twenty dollars a night, but the linen's clean."

"You've been there?"

"Half an hour ago," she said. "That's why I was late. I took one of the cabins, and I checked it just to make sure there wasn't a porcupine sitting on the bed. There could have been, but there wasn't."

A lot of things went through his mind. He picked one of them and said, "You didn't use a credit card."

"Of course not."

"Good."

His hand was on the table, next to the unfinished bottle of beer, and her hand settled on top of his.

"Afterwards," she said, "we'll be able to talk."

ELEVEN

He was sprawled out on his back, feeling like a puppet with its strings cut. His eyes were closed, and he had the sense that he could just float away, like a leaf on a stream.

She lay her hand on him, brushed her fingertips across the hair on his chest. She said, "We worked up a sweat, didn't we? I could put the air on."

"I'm comfortable."

"Well, I'm dripping, but that's your doing. You don't suppose we just got me pregnant, do you?"

"I never even thought."

"Now wouldn't that win the prize for ironic," she said, "after what George and I went through."

"He wanted a child?"

"Desperately, and if you ever met his kids, you'd have to wonder why. Two girls and a boy, and the older girl's the same age as I am."

"I know."

"The girls are bitches who hated me before they even met me, and Alden wouldn't know which to do first, fuck me or kill me. Both, if possible, and I don't think he'd much care about the order. You know about his kids?"

"Just that there are three of them, and the one girl's your age."

"You know a whole lot about me, don't you?" She moved her hand lower, curled her fingers around his penis. "It's so soft and small and harmless now," she said. "Just to lull a girl into feeling safe. Who are you, Doak?"

"A New York cop who figured his pension would go further in the Sunshine State."

"And it didn't go as far as you hoped, so you got sworn in as a deputy sheriff?"

He shook his head. "Got a private investigator's license, got to know the sheriff, and when he needed somebody with no local ties to play a part and wear a wire, I got the job."

"And that was when, a couple of days ago?"

"There was a job before that," he said, and started to tell her about the auto dealer. She remembered him, how he'd tried to get his partner killed and wound up going away for it, but hadn't known about the way the evidence was gathered to lock down the case.

"And that was you? Same as this morning, he got in the car with you and you got him to talk?"

"But he got to make up his own lines," he said. "They weren't all written down for him on a legal pad."

"Then you turned in the recording and collected your fee and he went off to prison. Was it a substantial fee?"

"Not especially."

"How about for me? Will they pay you even though I didn't say anything useful?"

"They'd pay for my time. I told them not to bother, that I was happy to do a favor for Gallatin County."

"And if it was all the same to them, you'd just as soon get paid in pussy. Oh, come *on*. Don't tell me you weren't expecting this."

"I suppose I was."

"I'd have to be grateful, wouldn't I? I was this close to getting locked up."

"You could have had a change of heart," he pointed out. "The lines I printed out for you? You could have come up with them on your own, and meant them."

"But that's not what would have happened."

"How can you know that for sure? We'll never know, because I didn't give you the chance to change your mind."

"And a good thing, Doak, because that wasn't gonna happen. What was it you said, when you pretended to try to talk me back into it? 'I bet you've got the thousand dollars in your purse.' Well, you're damn right I did, and that wasn't all I had. There was another envelope, a thicker one, with twenty thousand in it, because I knew you'd want half the money before you did the work, and I wanted to move right on to the next step."

"Who told you the price was going to be forty thousand?"

"Nobody. I was just guessing, and what I guessed was fifty, but twenty-five was more than I could come up with, it was a stretch to get my hands on twenty. And you know, a bird in the hand. Oh, that's an idea."

Her fingers found him again. "Now I've got your bird in my hand. Now you touch me. Put your finger in. Yes, that's nice. Let's not do anything, let's just go on conversating while we touch each other like this."

"Conversating?"

"Haven't you heard people say that? I love it, it's such a nice clunky word. Suppose the price was fifty thousand and you wanted half in advance, and all I could come up with was twenty. You'd have taken it, wouldn't you?"

"Wouldn't I have to be a hit man to answer that?"

"Yeah, it's a little too hypothetical, isn't it? What kind of name is Doak?"

"The only one anybody ever calls me."

"Somebody must call you Mr. Miller. That's the last name you said for the tape, and it would have to be your real name if you were preparing something for use as evidence in a murder trial. Except it wouldn't be murder unless you did it. What would I have been charged with?"

"Criminal solicitation to murder."

"I was arrested once for soliciting. Which was pure bullshit, because I was the one girl from Minnesota who got off the bus in Port Authority and didn't get turned out by a pimp."

"You came to New York?"

"I didn't stay long. The city scared the crap out of me. And the prices! Three, four days and I was back at Port Authority getting on another bus."

"But not back to Minnesota."

"No. How I got arrested, this cop in Houston hit on me and I wasn't interested. I was a barista in a place that wished it was Starbucks, and this creepy guy hit on me, which happened all the time, and I blew him off. And he showed me a badge."

"And arrested you?"

"Gave me a choice. 'You can suck my cock and I'll let you go, or I'll slap the cuffs on you and swear you *offered* to suck me off, and you'll say you didn't, and who do you think they'll believe?' Me, I thought, because everybody must know you're a lying sack of shit, and I held out my hands for the cuffs."

"And he laughed and let you go."

"No, I told you I got arrested. He put the cuffs on and told me I was under arrest and led me out of there, and when we got around the corner he laughed, like it was a big joke, and of course I didn't think he was serious, did I? And after he copped a feel he unlocked the handcuffs and told me I was free to go, and when I walked into the shop everybody stared at me."

"Jesus."

"I could have toughed it out, but for minimum wage? I decided the hell with the Coffee Clutch, and the hell with Houston, for that matter. Criminal solicitation to murder. That sounds serious."

"It's a step or two beyond littering."

"They'd have put me in jail, wouldn't they?"

"They'd have sent you to prison."

"But they won't, thanks to Mr. Miller. Doak Miller?"

"Right."

"You said some initials, and I don't believe either one of them was a D. One was a J, and I'm not sure of the other."

"J. W. Miller."

"Which one of them stands for Doak?"

"The W."

"You spell funny."

"My given name," he said, "is Jay Walker Miller."

"What's the J stand for? Mookie?"

"No, Jay's my first name, J-A-Y."

"Three letters, but it sounds the same as the one letter. That must be a pain in the ass, having to spell it out all the time."

"You got that right."

"I've known girls named Bea and Dee and Kaye, but those were nicknames for Beatrice and Dolores and Katherine, not actual official names. I still don't get how the W got to stand for Doak."

"It's not a very interesting story."

"Tell me anyway," she said, and gave him a gentle squeeze. "And how would it be if you put two fingers in? And you could move them around a little bit while you tell me."

"So you don't get bored."

"Oh, I won't get bored. I'm a long ways away from bored. Don't move your fingers too much, you don't have to stir me up, just…yeah, like that. That's kind of nice, moving them like that."

So he started talking, telling her how his name was Jay Walker Miller because that was how it worked in his family. His mother's maiden name was Marjorie Walker, so he got Walker for a middle name, and his father's name was Jay Prescott Miller, because

his father's *mother's* maiden name, which is to say his grand-
mother's name, was Juliana Prescott.

So he was a Jay, like his father, but not a Junior, because they
had different middle names. And it was actually a tradition that
went back a total of four or five generations, but it stopped with
him. He'd married a woman named Doreen Geoghegan, and he
was damned if he was going to saddle a kid with a middle name
no one was sure how to pronounce. The fucking Geoghegans
couldn't even agree on it, one branch of the family calling themselves GAY-gan, the others opting for Guh-HEE-gan. And nobody
ever called him Jay, and a name that sounded like an initial was a
pain in the ass anyway, so the hell with it. His son was Gary
Andrew Miller, and he'd spared the little prick a lifetime of
aggravation, and for what? The kid wouldn't speak to him.

"Why?"

"We'll get to that," he said. "Everybody called my father Jay,
so they had to call me something different, and they settled on
Walker. And then somebody, I think it was one of my uncles,
remembered a football player named Doak Walker. He was
a Texas kid who played for SMU, a three-time All-American.
ESPN put him fourth on the list of all-time great college football
players. Then he went on to play half a dozen seasons for the
Detroit Lions, and after he was through they retired his number."

"What was the number?"

"Thirty-seven. Why?"

"To see if you knew it. I'm sorry, keep talking. And keep,
um—"

"Doing this?"

"Yeah."

"I know a whole lot about Doak Walker, and I'm tempted to
tell you every last word of it because I don't ever want to take
my fingers out of you. Are you okay with that?"

"Uh-huh."

"I grew up thinking Doak was his nickname, same as it was mine, but one day I looked it up and found out his actual name was Ewell Doak Walker, Junior. So it was his real middle name, and it was his father's real middle name, and where it came from originally I have no idea. But I could make something up, just to keep on talking."

"Or you could forget him and tell me more about you."

"Or I could stop talking," he said, "and eat your pussy."

"Oh," she said. "Yes, you could do that."

He slid his hands under her buttocks and put his mouth on her and the world went away.

TWELVE

"Well, I think we've established that you can make me come."

"I almost didn't want you to," he said, "because then I'd have to stop."

"But you didn't stop, did you? Jesus Christ, you kept going and I kept coming. The Energizer Bunny, takes a ticking and keeps on licking."

"I think you just might have that backwards."

"And it's not the Bunny anyway, it's some other commercial."

"Timex watches."

"Okay. Okey dokey. Okey *Doak*-y, I mean. God, listen to me. Or don't listen to me. You know that expression, fucking somebody's brains out? I think that's what just happened to me."

"God, you're beautiful."

"Don't change the subject. You know what I still don't get? What it was that made you decide to sabotage the sheriff's sting. It can't be because you have a lot of trouble getting laid. I don't believe that for a minute."

"I know, it's a real problem. Women are after me all the time. My house is on a creek, but with a little digging I could extend it so that I had a moat around it."

"You've got a girlfriend, don't you?"

"There's one woman I see three or four times a month."

"Married, right? And she's the only one?"

"Sometimes I go out for a drink and I get lucky. But not all that often."

"And you don't look all that hard for it, either."

"No, I guess I don't. And no, I didn't write out a script for you last night because it was the best way I could think of to get laid."

"God, I hope not. Printing everything out by hand in big block capitals. I just know you've got a computer. You'd need it or how could you Google people like Doak Walker? Haven't you got a little old ink-jet printer to keep it company?"

"There's a record of everything you do on a computer."

"Even if you erase it?"

"I don't trust any of that. It gets on your hard drive and you think you've deleted it and it stores copies of itself in six different places. And some kid who drove his teachers nuts until they kicked his ass out of school, he sits down with the computer you scrubbed, and he can tell you what you had for breakfast and where you got your shoes."

"So you decided to be careful," she said. "I get it. I'm not used to thinking that way. I've never had to be careful before."

"You weren't very careful talking to Richard Gonson."

"No."

"You asked me a question, and I keep not answering it. I suppose I'm afraid of sounding like a moron. Well, too bad if I do. I'm going to tell you a fantasy I've had for over twenty years."

THIRTEEN

It was still full dark during the drive home, but the sky was starting to lighten up by the time he pulled into his driveway. He needed a shower, he'd driven all the way home smelling himself and smelling her on him, but when he got his clothes off he stretched out on the bed, just for a minute, and when he finally opened his eyes it was past noon.

He spent a long time in the shower, decided he didn't need to shave, but looked at himself in the mirror for a long moment. A little more gray at the temples, and he didn't mind it there, but knew it was the thin edge of the wedge. There'd be more gray coming.

He checked his phone. There was a call he had to return, from an insurance office in Perry that used him now and again for background checks. It didn't pay all that much, but he could generally get the job done without leaving his house, just noodling around a little on his computer.

Funny how computers had scared the crap out of him when they first started showing up at the station house. He'd thought of himself as an old-school cop, getting out in the city streets and knocking on doors, burning rubber, wearing out shoe leather. But the fear went away over time, and it turned out he had a natural affinity for the machine. The department would pay if you wanted to take a course on your own time, so he went to a third-floor room at John Jay three nights a week and let a young woman with a nose ring and a Hello Kitty tattoo turn him into an expert, though he didn't kid himself. He knew he was still nowhere near the proficiency level of the average twelve-year-old.

He returned the call, and the agent agreed to email him the applicant's name and vitals. The agent, Bob Newhouser, had played sports at Indian River State College in Fort Pierce, and now spent as much time as he could on the golf course. He liked golf jokes as much as he liked golf, and had a new one this morning, and Doak didn't have to force his laugh.

He booted up his computer, checked his email, deleted most of it. He stood up, realized he was hungry, and remembered emptying the milk carton over the last of the cereal. Was there anything in the refrigerator? Nothing but beer, and that wasn't how the day ought to start.

He checked his other phone. The new one.

Nothing.

He went out for breakfast.

They'd taken both cars from Kimberley's to the motel. She led in the Lexus and he followed her along the stretch of empty road, parked in the back near the cabin she'd rented.

And when it was time to go he'd stood in the cabin's doorway and watched her taillights disappear in the distance.

First, though, he'd given her a cell phone. He'd bought two of them for $39.99 apiece in a 7-Eleven on 41, paying cash and waving away the receipt. He'd tossed the packaging and instructions and programmed each with the phone number of the other.

And in the little Tourist Court cabin he'd given her one of them and showed her how it worked. "It's prepaid," he said, "with more message units than we're likely to use. You use it only to call me, and only on the number that it's already set to dial. Never call me on any other phone, and never call any other number from this phone, and—"

"I get it. It'll be in my purse, and I won't leave home without it. But I think I'll keep it turned off and just check it from time to time."

"That's what I intend to do."

"It's complicated, isn't it? I like your fantasy better. We just get in the car and disappear. But it wouldn't work, would it?"

"For days, maybe weeks. Even as a fantasy that was about as much mileage as I could get out of it. You know the first thing you said to me at Kimberley's?"

"I forget what it was."

" 'Now what?' "

"Was that what I said? Yes, I guess it was."

"A couple of days, a couple of weeks at the outside, and that's the question we'd both be asking, and neither one of us would be able to come up with an answer."

"You did make it sound good, though."

"Riding off into the sunset."

"I was about ready to do it. Not even go back to pack a bag."

"That's an important part of it, not wasting a minute. The clothes on our backs and nothing else."

"Not bad. How many years did you run that tape?"

"Maybe twenty. Maybe more. You're the only person who ever got to hear it."

"I think I knew that. And now—"

"Now it's gone," he said.

"Did I do something to spoil it?"

He shook his head. "What killed it was hearing myself say the words. See, it's a fantasy about running, about a new start in a new place. The partner's just a reason to run and start over."

"In other words, a geographical solution."

"Which is how the West was won, you know. A whole swarm of malcontents telling themselves that the next place would be better."

"Makes me think of my mama and the losers she kept hooking up with. And me, for Christ's sake, playing hopscotch with a map of America."

"I came to Florida for a new start. And found it, fair enough, but I took myself along."

"Hard not to, isn't it? I make that little mistake every time. Doak, if your fantasy's dead, where do we go from here?"

" 'Now what.' "

"Yeah, that's still the question, isn't it? More than ever." She tilted her head, showed him the blue of her eyes. "I guess we'll have to look for the answer."

He drove to the Denny's on the motel strip outside of Perry, because they served breakfast around the clock, but when he looked at the menu he decided what he really wanted was a patty melt and an order of onion rings.

There was a 7-Eleven next door, but it was the one where he'd paid cash for the two cell phones. There'd be a different clerk at this hour, and nobody would bother to look at him twice, but it was just as easy to drive to the next convenience store on the strip for a box of cereal and a quart of milk and the couple of other things he'd run low on. He found enough items to get over the store's credit card minimum, and used his Visa, because another thing he was running low on was cash.

Back at his computer, he spent an hour checking out Raymond Fred Gartner, who'd been persuaded to insure his life for half a million dollars, with the benefit doubled in the event of accidental death.

Double indemnity, in other words, and that made him think of the movie, and that made him think of Lisa.

He finished his work on Gartner, and if there was any reason to turn down his application, he couldn't see what it might be. As far as he could tell, the most interesting thing about the man was his middle name, which was in fact Fred and not Frederick or Alfred or some other more formal equivalent.

He could have written up his report on the spot, he had all the data he needed, but a certain boots-on-the-ground presence made a good impression. So he got in the car and drove to the address he had for Raymond Fred.

Why not either Raymond Frederick or Ray Fred? Full names all the way or get all good-old-boy and pair the nicknames cracker-style, as in Joe Bob and Billy Ray…

He managed to find Gartner's address and circled the block, fair-sized ranch houses on landscaped lots, a suburban neighborhood in keeping with the sense of Gartner his computer had furnished. It wouldn't surprise him to know that the average homeowner carried a policy along the lines of what Newhouser had sold Gartner.

Of course, Bob Newhouser already knew all this, and had very likely been inside of Gartner's house instead of merely assessing its curb appeal in passing. So he could have skipped this part altogether, or stayed home and let Google Earth do the heavy lifting.

But knocking on doors, that was something you had to do in person.

And so he pulled up in front of the house to the immediate left of Gartner's and went to the front door, carrying the clipboard that always went with him on such excursions. Not because he was much at jotting things down, but because nothing equaled a clipboard for establishing one as being a legitimate man of purpose.

There was a yellow pad under the clip, the one he'd used to write out that little one-act radio play starring Doak and Lisa. The sheets he'd covered with block capitals had all been shredded, along with the several blank sheets at the top of the pad, where the pressure of the ballpoint might have left a lasting impression.

Because you couldn't be too careful.

Once he'd knocked on a door on the top floor of a Brownsville tenement, and something made him step aside just seconds before a bullet came through it. From that time on he always stood to the side of the door when he knocked, and of course he never saw another bullet.

Another time, a woman answered the door wearing bunny slippers and nothing else. She had a drink in her hand and, he suspected, quite a few others inside her. He had a partner with him, a kid named Birch who'd just made the move to plainclothes, and it was interesting to watch him work at keeping his composure.

He'd heard squad room stories of similar situations, and in some of the stories the responding officers did the right thing, feeding the poor dear a couple of aspirin and tucking her into her solitary bed. And in other stories the officers responded in a more assertive fashion, treating their hostess to a two-on-one.

Either ending was plausible, he supposed. He and Birch had taken a middle course, just turning around and getting the hell out of there. Years later he'd run into Birch, who asked if he remembered the naked lady with the bunny slippers (he could hardly have forgotten her) and wondering what had ever become of her. He had no idea.

"She had a shaved bush," Birch said. "Never saw one of those before."

Had she? He couldn't remember that part.

"Now it's all the rage, I guess. You know, man, we could of taken her in the bedroom and done anything we fuckin' wanted to her."

"I guess."

"Say we do it. You think she's gonna mind? Probably wants it, or at least half of her wants it."

"The top half or the bottom half?"

"The shaved half. I mean, who comes to the fucking door like that? And what's the odds she's even gonna remember it the next day? 'Oh, goodness, my pussy's sore. I must have fucked a couple of cops.' What's the matter, Doak?"

"Nothing," he'd said, "but you were what, twenty-two when I knew you? Twenty-three?"

"So?"

"So you've changed some since then."

"Well, this fucking job," Burke said. "And anyway, who's the same person he was at twenty-three? Who in his right mind would want to be?"

Since then, just as no one had fired through a door at him, neither had anyone shown up in bunny slippers. But, even as he stood to the side of the door (even here in this placid suburb, where people didn't shoot through doors) so too did he allow himself the wistful thought that the door might open onto an adventure, a brief encounter.

What did he need, or even want, with the kind of adventure that might wait behind a closed door? He was in the middle of an adventure with, literally, the girl of his dreams, and he had another very adventurous lady as a Friend with Benefits. Was he turning out to be just like the mopes on *Let's Make a Deal*, jumping up and down because they'd just won the prize of a lifetime, then ready to throw it away for whatever might turn out to be behind Door Number Three?

He had time to think this over, because nobody came to the door at first, and if he hadn't seen the squareback Honda in the driveway, he'd have tried his luck next door. But he gave it another minute, and heard footsteps and muted conversation, and then the door was opened by a woman in a pastel print housedress. She had a toddler clinging to her hand, a little boy with white-blond hair, and her shape suggested that he could expect a brother or sister in two or three months.

He gave her his name, told her the man next door had applied for an insurance policy and he needed to confirm a couple of points. In the living room, he asked her half a dozen innocuous questions to which he already knew the answers, then moved on to get a more personal perspective. What kind of neighbor was Ray Gartner? His lawn and yard looked good today, but was that generally the case? What was her impression of the Gartners' marriage? Did they entertain a lot? Keep late hours? Have loud arguments?

He barely paid attention to her answers, which were everything both Gartner and his prospective insurers could have hoped for. Instead he found himself increasingly aware of the woman's body. Her son sat beside her, turning the pages of a picture book about dinosaurs, while his mommy testified to the laudable ordinariness of the family next door.

A Milf, that was the term for her. An acronym of the texting generation, for a Mother I'd Like to Fuck. Make that an eMilf, he thought, with the E for Expectant.

How long since he'd had a pregnant woman? Ages, he realized, because he'd never had one aside from Doreen, not that he was ever aware of. And if any of their couplings during either of her pregnancies had been notable, they were so no longer. He couldn't remember them. He knew they'd had sex while she was pregnant, though not terribly often, but had there been anything different about it?

What would it be like with this one?

Her name was Roberta Ellison, he'd had to write it down for

his report. *Roberta, I think pregnancy is making your breasts swell up, because your maternity housedress is getting too tight on top. Roberta, I bet your husband's too gentle with you these days, I bet he's afraid he'll hurt either you or the baby. Roberta, I won't make that mistake, because I don't care if it hurts you, I don't care if it fucking kills your baby.*

Did she have any idea what he was thinking?

She was probably thirty or close to it, but she wasn't wearing any makeup and her face was an oval with small regular features, and she looked younger than her years.

He said, "Well, I think that'll do it. You've been very helpful, and I don't think your neighbor has anything to worry about. Thanks very much for your time, Mrs. Ellison."

FOURTEEN

Back at his house, he typed up his report, including a summary of his interview with one *Roberta Ellison, neighbor*, and printed it out. He could have attached it to an email, but Bob Newhouser was an old-school hard-copy kind of a guy. He liked everything on paper so he could slip it into a manilla file folder and tuck it away in a steel cabinet, so Doak printed out two copies, one for Newhouser and one for his own files, not that he ever expected to look at it again. If he ever needed to see what he'd written, which was doubtful, he'd find the document on his hard drive. That had to be easier than rooting around in the cardboard carton that served him as an unclassified file cabinet.

He'd been checking the new phone periodically, and he checked it now, and this time he had a voicemail. It had come in just minutes ago. He played it, and heard her say, "Call me."

He erased the message first, then made the call. She answered at once. She said, "Is it you? 'Cause this is me."

"I somehow figured as much."

"Do we need code names? Maybe not, if we're the only two people who ever use either of these phones. I want you to know I have no idea what I'm doing here. Is it safe to talk on these things?"

"Where are you?"

"At the Baron. I'm early for my shift, I'm out back in my car. Well, leaning against my car."

"Parked up against the building?"

"No, I'm at the back of the lot. If you're thinking security cameras, we've got one, but I'm in its blind spot. If you're impressed, don't be. It's my usual spot."

"I'm impressed anyway," he said. "Outside is good. I'm in my house—"

"Not out on the dock?"

"No, although that's not a bad idea. In a little while maybe I'll crack a beer and go out there."

"I wish I could join you."

"I don't think—"

"Oh, it's not the kind of wish you have to steer me away from. It's like I wish dogs could talk so you could have real conversations with them."

"One of the best things about them," he said, "is they can't."

"See, now *that* wasn't a wish you had to steer me away from, either, and now you ruined it for me. I'll never be able to wish it again."

"I'm sorry."

"I should hope you are. I couldn't come over even if it was a good idea, because I'm about to start my shift and watch otherwise prudent men defy their cardiologists. Are you okay, darling? Is everything good?"

"Yes and yes."

"I just called you darling."

"I know."

"Am I still your fantasy girl? Or did that go up in smoke along with the fantasy?"

"Oh, you're it," he said.

"God, I like the way you said that. It gave me a little shiver. What did you do today? And if that's a terrible question, you've got to admit it's better than *What are you wearing*."

"Some work for an insurance company. Most of it on the computer, going into some subscription databases, but then I drove over and looked at his house and interviewed the lady next door."

"Was that fun?"

"She was pregnant, and a very well-behaved little boy sat on the couch next to her."

"It's good the kid's well behaved, or she'd be sick at the prospect of having another."

"I wanted to fuck her."

"Really."

"Yeah, I really did. I sat there asking stupid who-gives-a-shit questions and pretending to pay attention to her answers, and I wanted the kid to go into the other room so I could fuck his mother."

"But you didn't do anything, or say anything."

"No. I hadn't planned on mentioning it."

"Yet here you are, telling me about it."

"Yeah, and I've got to be at least as surprised as you are. And I'm not trying to make you jealous—"

"Which I'm not."

"—or excited."

"Which I am, kind of. Anyway, I think I know why you're telling me."

"Oh?"

"Yeah. When I woke up this morning, I didn't give George a blow job."

"Now there's a coincidence," he said, "because neither did I."

"Just one more thing we've got in common, my darling. But, you know, I thought about it, because the occasional BJ makes life at home a good deal more tolerable for me."

"For him too, I bet."

"But here's the thing, when I thought about it I thought about you, and it struck me that if I blew George, or even if I just thought about blowing him, it didn't have to be a fucking secret. I could tell you. And I can, can't I?"

"Yes, of course."

"I can tell you absolutely everything. I'm still getting used to the idea, but it's true, isn't it?"

"Yes."

"And you told me about Mommy Preggers because you could. You could tell me how you wanted to fuck her, and if you actually did fuck her you could tell me that, too. We can tell each other anything. Isn't that amazing?"

"It is."

"Have you ever had anything like that with anybody?"

"Never. Have you?"

"Are you kidding? I've been nothing but secrets all my life. Are you gonna call her?"

"Call who? Oh, Roberta?"

"Is that her name, the pregnant lady?"

"Roberta Ellison."

"What does she look like? I want to picture her." He described the woman. "She sounds nice. You still want to fuck her, don't you?"

"I could live just fine without it," he said. "But would I like to fuck her? Which is not to say that I could, because she has a say in the matter, but yes, I'd like to."

"Well, you know where she lives. Give her a day or two and then drop by with some follow-up questions."

"Maybe."

"How would you do it?"

"How?"

"What position? You want to know what I think? I think you should take her from behind, with both of you lying on your sides, and you've got your arms around her so you can put your hands on her belly. What do you think of that?"

"If we by some chance got you pregnant last night," he said, "I think that'll eventually be a dandy position for us."

"Oh my God," she said. "I'd managed to forget about that. And now it's too late for a Morning After pill, and I don't have one, anyway. I'm not pregnant. I can't be, can I?"

"Probably not."

"Oh, look at the time. I got here way early and I'm gonna walk in late. And we're using up phone minutes, and what happens when we run out?"

"If we can't get them refilled, we'll just get new phones."

"Well, that's good to know," she said. "It's a big relief, actually. Because now I know we've got nothing to worry about."

After she ended the call, he sat for a long moment, letting it replay itself in his mind. He remembered the first mention of Lisa, in Radburn's office, the first glimpse of her on the sheriff's phone. Some bell had rung inside him at that first sight of her, but did it go back further than that? Hadn't he begun anticipating all of this even before he'd seen her picture?

And it kept building. Just now, the things she'd said to him, the things he'd found himself able to say to her. It was powerfully sexual, and yet from another angle it had next to nothing to do with sex.

All that crap lovers spouted in the movies, finding one's other self, being two halves of the same person. It had never quite made sense to him, and he wasn't sure it did now, and those weren't the words he'd use if he found himself moved to talk about it. But he knew what they were getting at, the writers who put those lines in the characters' mouths.

He had the refrigerator door half open and changed his mind, went back to his desk. Opened up Google, typed *george otterbein*, hit Enter.

FIFTEEN

His browser was Firefox, and it had a pull-down menu called History. He selected *Clear Recent History*, and it wanted him to say for how long. One hour? Two hours? It was getting on for seven o'clock, and he wasn't sure when he'd started. *Last Hour. Last Two Hours. Last Four Hours. Today. Everything.*

Probably two hours, he thought, but he selected *Last Four Hours* and wiped away that much of the recent past.

Then he went and got that beer from the fridge and took it out onto the dock.

He thought about Roberta Ellison, with her round belly and her swelling tits, and about the conversation she'd inspired.

"You should take her from behind, with both of you lying on your sides, and you've got your arms around her so you can put your hands on her belly…"

Got him hard, talking like that, but it was very different from the phone sex with Barb Hamill. That had been stimulating because stimulation was its whole purpose, its sole reason for being. Their words had been selected for erotic effect, to get them going and get them off, and it had worked for Barb and would have worked for him if his body hadn't chosen to hold itself back.

Saving the money shot for Lisa.

He'd have to tell Lisa about Barb. He'd mentioned her—that there was a married woman he was seeing casually, but he'd have to tell her about the sex, the phone sex and the bedroom sex.

Would he keep seeing Barb? He'd met the love of his life,

he'd finally encountered Fantasy Girl and had found with her something that went way beyond his fantasies, so why would he want to go on seeing Barb?

Because she was hot, he thought. Because it was a joy to pose her on her knees and moisten himself in one of her openings so he could slip into the other one, fucking her gorgeous heart-shaped ass and making her like it.

He wished she would call. It wasn't going to happen, she only called during the daytime, but he wished she'd call right now and come over right now so he could fuck her.

And the best part would be later, when he told Lisa about it.

Kinky, he thought, but it wasn't just kinky. It was more than kinky. It was…well, he didn't know what it was, exactly.

He found himself thinking, for the first time in years, of Phyllis Arenbeck. She was a tiny brown-haired creature, built like a boy, and married to Red Arenbeck, a uniformed cop built like a tight end. He had in fact played that position at Long Island University, and he'd been big enough for the NFL, but nowhere near good enough. He was bigger as a cop than he'd been as a football player, packing fat on top of muscle, and there was a Mutt and Jeff aspect to the Arenbecks as a couple.

He knew Red from the job, but not well, and he'd met Phyllis a couple of times at parties. Then there was an engagement party for a mutual acquaintance at somebody's house in Ridgewood, and he was fixing himself a drink he didn't particularly need when Phyllis joined him.

She said, "Cops. You wouldn't believe how many of 'em hit on me in the past what, two hours?"

"I'd believe it."

"Oh yeah? Come on, I'm nothing special. I'm a skinny little thing with a flat chest."

"All the same," he said, "you're hot."

"You didn't hit on me."

"I thought about it," he said. He hadn't, but it was something to say, and he'd no sooner said it than he felt her hand on his crotch, copping a quick feel.

"Okay," she said softly, letting go of him and moving to the side. "The guest bathroom's off the kitchen. Lock the door and wait."

She kept him waiting just long enough to suspect she'd probably thought better of it, and then there was a quiet knock on the door. "It's me," she said, and he opened the door. She slipped in, turned the lock, and got up on her tiptoes for a kiss. She'd been drinking something sweet and her mouth tasted of it, and when he put his tongue in her mouth she sucked on it, and he thought, Jesus, is this happening? In a fucking bathroom?

Then her hand was on his crotch, only this time she was lowering his zipper and taking what she wanted.

She said, "Oh, good. You're circumcised."

"I didn't know you were Jewish."

"I'm not," she said. "I'm just particular about what I put in my mouth."

Phyllis, skinny little thing, no tits, no ass, and none of that mattered.

"Choke me, will you? Come on, how tricky is that? Use both hands, put 'em around my throat, and choke me a little. Not too hard. Oh, that's nice. A little harder, just a little bit. Oh, yeah."

Weird, that part. He'd have to tell Lisa, wondered what she would make of it.

He finished the beer, thought about getting another, found it easier to stay where he was, looking out at the water. Found it too easy to stay there, he knew, and he couldn't stay there much longer, because with the sun down the bugs would be coming around soon. So many of the little bastards with nothing better to do than fly around looking for somebody to bite.

Time to shut off the flow of memories. Time to get off his ass and do something.

George and Lisa Otterbein lived in a three-story house built of quarried stone and located exactly a mile and a half north of the Belle Vista town line. The house was at the top of a rise, a feature less common in Florida than elsewhere, and a white rail fence girdled the eight-acre property. The house could have been plucked from one of those sleepy villages along the Delaware, in Bucks County, Pennsylvania, say, or New Jersey's Hunterdon County. And the rail fence put you in mind of horse farms in Kentucky, and a mint julep in a frosty glass.

There was a good-sized pond, too, and trees, live oak and sweetgum, dripping with Spanish moss.

He didn't stop, but slowed down as he drove past the place. Place? The Otterbein Estate, that's what it was, and yes, he was impressed. Who wouldn't be?

George had lived here with Jo, had raised his kids here, and moved Lisa into the house when he married her. Doak had heard tell of second wives who bridled at the idea of moving into another woman's house, but he figured it might depend on the house. A three-bedroom cube in Levittown was one thing, a stone mansion was a whole nother story.

She must have felt like a queen here. Or a princess, given the age difference. A princess living in a palace, that's how she would have felt.

Until she didn't.

A princess in a tower, and instead of letting down her long black hair she'd cut it off and gone back to work. And one night she'd picked out a man with a raffish reputation and asked him to hook her up with a murderer.

And so on.

A hell of a way for a girl to meet her soul mate, her other half.

He pointed the Monte Carlo away from Chez Otterbein, drove without paying much attention to the route he was taking. Jesus, the damn fantasy, two lovers sufficiently besotted with each other to walk away from everything they had. Easy for him to spin that yarn, because what did he ever have that it would pain him to walk away from? A low-rent house he never cared about, a low-rent life that was no pleasure to live. And a wife he couldn't stand—and, it had turned out, who couldn't stand him, either.

Who could expect a woman like Lisa to walk away from that big pile of stone? Who in his right mind would ask her to head out for the territories in his broken-down Chevy? Never mind that she drove a Lexus. He'd be willing to bet there were at least five other vehicles garaged at the Otterbein estate, and even the riding mower had to be worth more than the piece of shit he was driving.

Go ahead, try to picture her in the house on Osprey Drive. Once, maybe, before George Otterbein, before the stone house, before all the money. If the timing had been different, if their paths had crossed before she ever met the old man, before she got used to a life he'd never be able to afford. Maybe the same chemistry that worked for them now would have been there in that alternate universe, and they could work side by side at the kitchen table. She could keep the books and send out invoices, and he could teach her the handful of skills and street knowledge you needed in his business. Hell, she'd be a natural at undercover work, and she'd enjoy it, learn to make a game of it. Miller & Yarrow, Confidential Investigations…

Yeah, right.

It was hard enough to bring the image into focus, and that was before you reminded yourself it could never have happened because the timing could never have been right. It had taken every bit of his past and every bit of hers to bring them here now at the same time, at what was probably the only moment of their mutual lives when they were ready for each other.

And consider this. If that was what she'd wanted, a love match that partnered her with a guy who had to work for a living, she'd have found it a lot sooner in her hopscotch pilgrimage from Minnesota to Florida.

With her looks, her manner, she'd never have been involuntarily alone. She'd have had men around her all the time. She wouldn't have had any trouble finding one to marry her.

The one she found was George Otterbein. And he might be twice her age, but that didn't mean he'd snatched her from the cradle. She'd lived more than a handful of years, a grown woman on her own, before Otterbein came into the picture.

Picture Lisa Yarrow on Osprey Drive?

No, I don't think so. But what if you flip the negative.

Could you picture Doak Miller leaning back in a recliner on a couple of acres of lawn? With a big stone house behind him, and a pond, and a rail fence?

How would that strike the eye?

SIXTEEN

Things to do.

He stopped at an ATM, got some cash. Drove south and east for half an hour, slowed down, and passed four motels before he found one that looked right.

He pulled up in front of the office. He saw a security camera positioned above the entrance, but they were everywhere these days, and he'd be a long time finding a motel without one. He reached into the backseat for a ball cap, wore it low over his eyes.

The woman behind the counter was chewing gum. If it was to keep her awake, well, that was a lot to expect from a strip of Juicy Fruit. She was long and lean and wasted, with bad skin and bad tattoos, a played-out tweaker who could only have been hired by an incurable optimist. Or a relative, hoping Florrie Mae could just put in her hours without giving the store away or burning it down.

He was looking for a room for a week, he said. Something in the back, something quiet.

She said they did, and quoted him a day rate. He reminded her he'd want it by the week. Be seven times the day rate, she said, and he pointed out that the sign out front offered weekly rates. She frowned and picked up the phone, relaying the inquiry to someone in another part of the unit, then bounced the answer back to him.

"You'd have to pay in advance. Pay for six days, get one for free. Sixty a night times six…"

"That's three-sixty," he said.

"Plus the tax."

"Make it three-fifty even," he said, "and forget the tax, and I'll give you seven hundred now for the next two weeks."

He figured anybody would say yes to that, and he'd have paid cash anyway, but this gave him a dollars-and-cents reason to pay cash, and gave the owner a reason to keep the whole thing off the books. She checked with whoever was on the other end of the phone, and nodded as she replaced the receiver.

"Be fine," she said, and put a key on the counter. "So that's seven hundred dollars plus—no, sorry, not plus anything. Just seven hundred dollars."

There was a registration card to fill out. He'd already decided to be Martin Williams from Brunswick, Georgia. There was a place for the car's tag number, and he used his own tag with a couple of numbers reversed, and indicated it was a Georgia license.

She could have asked to see a driver's license. He had a reasonable assortment of fake ID, some of it pretty convincing, but none of it with Martin Williams's name on it, none of it licensing its possessor to operate a motor vehicle in the state of Georgia. So if she asked for ID he'd have had to feign indignation and march on out of there, repeating his act at the next suitable motel down the road.

But why would she ask to see his license? It's not as if he'd asked to borrow her car. And she spent all her working hours checking in people unlikely to give their real names, let alone carry ID to back them up.

"I got a few weeks work in the area," he told her, "and the schedule's crazy, so I'll be keeping odd hours. I wouldn't want the maid coming in while I'm sleeping."

"You put out the doughnut," she said, "and won't nobody disturb you unless the building's on fire."

"The doughnut?"

She rolled her eyes. "The sign, Do Not Disturb. You hang it on the doorknob. Don't y'all call that a doughnut?"

"Never used to," he said, "but I guess I will from now on."

The room was about what you'd expect. The TV was small, and fifteen or twenty years old, and mounted so high on the wall you'd get a stiff neck watching it, but he hadn't booked the place so they could watch Vanna White earn big bucks turning letters. The walls sported fake wood-grain paneling, and the toilet had a strip fastened around the seat, announcing that it had been sanitized for his protection. He'd have found that more reassuring if it had also been flushed, but someone had missed that particular step. He flushed it, and determined that it was at least in working order. That was something.

The dresser bore several scars from unattended cigarettes, and the drapes held the smell of cigarette smoke. He'd never thought to ask for a non-smoking room, and then he saw the sign: this *was* a non-smoking room. That explained the absence of ashtrays, which in turn explained the burns on the dresser— and, he noted, on the bedside tables as well.

The bed was all right. There was decent water pressure in the shower. For the next two weeks the room was theirs, and they could come and go as they pleased without showing themselves at the front desk.

Quite a contrast, though, with Chez Otterbein. Except a French word like *chez* didn't really go with a Teutonic name like Otterbein. *Haus* was the German word for house, or at least it ought to be, but Haus Otterbein didn't really cut the *moutarde*.

The doughnut was reversible, Do Not Disturb on one side, with a cartoon drawing of a man sleeping; Please Make Up This

Room on the other, with a drawing of a chambermaid fluffing a pillow. It was hard to imagine anybody fluffing a pillow in this room.

He hung the doughnut on the knob, pulled the door shut, checked that the lock had engaged, and got in his car and left.

Ten miles north on 19, he stopped at a Waffle House for eggs and hash browns and coffee. He checked the new phone, the Lisa phone. No messages, so he called and left one: *Call me when you can.*

When he got home he took a shower. He checked his phone, but she hadn't called back. He set it so that it would ring if she did, and put it down on the table next to the computer.

Checked his email, checked the news headlines, checked a few websites he kept up with.

Went to Google Translate. Ah, gotcha. Schloss.

Schloss Otterbein. Meaning castle, palace, chateau, manor house, or stately home. Perfect, he thought, and the phone rang, the Lisa phone.

"Schloss Otterbein," he said.

And heard nothing but silence. Oh, Jesus, he thought. What did he get, a wrong number? Or worse, if someone had picked up her phone and tried to see what it was programmed to call.

Then, tentatively, she said, "Now what."

"It's me."

"I figured that out, but it gave me a turn. What was that word you said before my name?"

"Schloss," he said, and explained its meaning. "It was no way to answer the phone, and I apologize, but I was sitting here congratulating myself for finding the right word, and right at that minute the phone rang, and, well…"

"I was expecting voicemail, and instead I heard my name. It was so unexpected it didn't register that it was your voice. You're home?"

"At the computer, looking up the name of your house. My name for it, that is. Does it have a name? Like The Breakers or, I don't know—"

"Dunrovin? Always a popular favorite. No, it doesn't have a name. That's the one thing about George's rock pile that's not pretentious."

"I guess you wouldn't mistake it for a Fleetwood Double-Wide."

"You've seen it?"

"From the street, at twenty miles an hour. A few hours ago."

"Was that—"

"Safe? I didn't ring the doorbell. I didn't even hit the brakes. I was just doing a little light reconnaissance. Then I set out on an important mission."

"Oh?"

"I rented us a love nest."

"Seriously?"

"It'll remind you of Tourist Court, with a little less in the way of rustic charm. But we're paid in advance for the next two weeks, with nobody near us to see us or hear us."

"Where is it?"

"You know where Cross City is?"

"I think I've driven through it."

"If you drove south on 19 you'd hit it, and you'd probably drive through it, because there's no reason to stop. Or at least there wasn't until now."

"Right. That's from a song, isn't it? Nobody near us."

"To see us or hear us. *Tea for Two*."

"I wasn't paying attention, but it must have stuck in my mind and I was hearing the music. Honey, I can't go there now. Another late night's not gonna work for me."

"I wasn't about to suggest it."

"Oh, that's good, because right now all I want to do is go home."

"Understood."

"I mean, that's not what I *want* to do, but it's what I'd really better do."

"I was thinking daytime," he said. "Late morning or early afternoon, when you'd naturally be out shopping or doing wifey-type things."

"Wifey-type things."

"Maybe not the best way to put it, but—"

"No, I was just thinking how day after day of wifey-type things made my old job look real good to me. Wifey-type things got me back to work."

"And made you cut your hair."

She was silent for a moment. Then she said, "You know my hair used to be long."

"Radburn mentioned it. And Google Images has pictures of you with long hair."

"Really? On the internet?"

"You and George at a benefit for some disease I never heard of."

"Oh, I know the one you mean, and I can't think of the name of it. Very rare, but this couple had a kid that died of it, so that became their cause. And everybody supports everybody else's cause, so that everybody'll have something to do on a Saturday night. Of course I had to buy a dress for the occasion. You always do, and then you're sort of committed to donate at least as much as you spent on the dress."

"You were wearing your hair down."

"Yes," she said. "And now it's short, and I'm going to tell you why I cut it, but not now."

"Okay."

"I want very much to tell you, darling, but not over the phone. Because I might need your arms around me, either while I'm telling you or afterward."

"Both, if you want."

"Both arms? Oh, both as in both during and after. I'm a little brain dead, I want to get my body under a shower and then into bed. My head on a pillow, and if I'm lucky I'll dream about you. Will you dream about me?"

"It'll be wasted if I do. I never remember my dreams."

"Never? I'd be glad to miss some of my dreams, but the good ones are sweet. I'll have a sweet dream about you and tomorrow —oh, *shit*."

"Tomorrow's a problem?"

"Tomorrow's what, Friday? It's not a problem, it's just purely impossible. But Saturday's good. The whole morning's free and half of the afternoon, until my shift starts at the restaurant. Can we wait until then?"

"Sure."

"I'll call you Saturday morning. What I won't do is call you tomorrow, unless there's a major problem. And don't call me, either. Tomorrow your assignment is to get into some mischief with one of your girlfriends, the pregnant one or the married one. Except the pregnant one is married, too, isn't she?"

"And so are you."

"I was just about to say that. What is it with Doak and married ladies? The one who's not pregnant, she's the one who sold you your house, right? Am I remembering correctly?"

"You are."

"On Osprey Drive. I don't care which one you fuck tomorrow,

just so you show up at our little love nest with a story to tell me."

"And you'll tell me about the haircut."

"Oh, I will," she said. "That may not be quite as much fun, but I'll tell you."

SEVENTEEN

In the morning he called Bob Newhouser and caught him at his desk. "I'm putting my report in the mail," he said. "If there's anything wrong with Raymond Fred Gartner, it flew under my radar. He comes up lily-white on all my databases, and the neighbor lady gives him a clean bill of health."

"I'm not surprised. I've played golf with him, and you get a pretty good sense of a fellow when you're out in the sun for eighteen holes. Oh, here's one you'll like."

It was a golf story, and one Newhouser had already told him, but it was no great hardship to hear it again. Doak furnished the requisite laugh, and Newhouser asked if the neighbor lady was anybody he might know.

"Probably," he said. "Is there anybody in Gallatin County you don't know?"

"Oh, there's a few."

"This one's a nice proper suburban mommy. Name's in the report, along with being on the tip of my tongue."

"Hell of a place for it."

"Roberta," he said. "Roberta Ellison."

"Roberta Ellison. Roberta Ellison." Then the penny dropped. "Oh, Jesus," Newhouser said. "Bobbie Jondahl. She married a guy named Ellison, and I could probably come up with his first name if I had to, but I can't think of a reason to waste any of my remaining brain cells on it."

"You want to hang on to the ones you've got left."

"Amen to that, brother Doak. He's from somewhere up in the Panhandle, came down to go to work at Zebulon Industries.

Knocked up Bobbie Jondahl and married her, and I gather he's had the good sense to keep her barefoot and pregnant ever since."

"She's pregnant even as we speak."

"Little Bobbie. Looks like butter wouldn't melt in her mouth, and you can finish that sentence on your own."

Well, that was interesting.

He weighed his options. One, he could pick up his clipboard and try to time his visit to the young Master Ellison's nap time, whenever that might be. Two, he could take a proactive approach to his Friendship with Benefits and call Barb. Three, he could stay at his computer and do a little more research, because you never knew what you might need to know.

An hour later he was in the Mykonos Diner, sitting across the table from Sheriff William Radburn.

"I somehow missed breakfast," Radburn said, "which is an oversight that needs to be corrected. You sure you won't have something?"

"Just coffee."

"Why I called, I been thinking some about our girl."

"Our girl. That would be —"

"Oh, why mention a name in a public place? We'll call her the lady who exercised the female prerogative and changed her mind."

"Okay."

"And there's no question she did just that, because I heard her say so loud and clear on the tape you brought in. You know, I played that some more."

"Oh?"

"I asked myself, Billy, is that a change of heart you're hearing?

And what I decided is it's not. So I got hold of another man whose name I won't mention just now, but he's the one told us about the little lady in the first place. Got the ball rolling, is what he did."

Richard Gonson.

"Now on the tape, she says she went back to him and tried to call it off, and he said it was out of his hands."

"I remember. He told her she could just not show up."

"Which, if you think about it, is what she should have done. Why keep a date with some homicidal Yankee if she was just gonna tell him to forget the whole thing? Only reason I can think of is to keep her options open, give herself a chance to decide at the last minute. Stand to reason?"

"I guess."

"You have to wonder who it was first came up with the idea of link sausages. I don't guess they give out Nobel prizes for that sort of thing, but the least you could have is a statue of him somewhere. But back to our friend."

"The man who started it all."

"Well, I'd have to say she's the one started it, but he's the one brought us into it. I asked him about this last conversation, the one where she asks him to hit the Undo button."

"It never happened?"

"Nope. Not to say you can take this fellow's word to the bank, but why would he lie about it?"

"Well, if she did have that conversation with him, and then he didn't bother to pass the word to us…"

"Point taken. Still, I got the impression this was the absolute first time he was hearing about calling things off."

"Which would reinforce your idea that she was keeping options open, and didn't completely change her mind until she got into my car. You think it was the car that queered the deal?"

" 'Guy can't afford a better car than this, how can you trust him to get away with murder?' Next time maybe we'll put you in a more suitable vehicle. If you hadn't helped put a perfectly good automobile dealer in Raiford, I bet he could help us out. You want a refill on the coffee?"

"No, I'm good."

"What I'm thinking, her calling it off don't convince me she's in love with her husband all over again. Who's to say she doesn't still want him dead?"

He didn't much like where this was going. But if the sheriff was thinking along these lines, he was just as glad he got to hear it. "There must be a whole lot of women who'd just as soon be widows," he said. "And husbands who'd love to be single again without the expense of divorce. What's the line? 'You can't always get what you want.' "

"You're saying there's a big difference between having an urge and acting on it."

"Isn't there? What percentage of people take the action?"

"But she already took it. Slued away at the last minute, but until then she was on board. I'll grant you there's a chance she genuinely changed her mind, but there's at least as good a chance she didn't."

"Meaning?"

"Meaning maybe she called you off because she found some-body else she was more comfortable working with. Her boy-friend, say."

"She's got a boyfriend?"

"That shocks you? 'By God, it's not bad enough she wants to kill her husband, but don't tell me she'd go so far as to cheat on him!' "

"Nobody mentioned a boyfriend," he said. "That's all. Has she got one?"

"That's something we ought to know, wouldn't you say? I was thinking there ought to be a way for you to earn some Gallatin County dollars."

"You want me to find out if she's got a boyfriend."

"Be good to know, Doak. Be good to see what else you can find out about her. Now you're the one person who can't sit down and interrogate her, on account of she already knows you as Jersey City Frank. You're shaking your head."

"For no good reason," he admitted. "Jersey City's in Hudson County, and we've been saying Frank's from—"

"Bergen County, and isn't that what they call a distinction that's not a difference? Never mind, I stand corrected. The point is you can't ask her questions. In fact you'd best keep your distance from the woman."

"That was my intention."

"But you can still dig around without getting into her field of vision, can't you? I don't want to use one of my men, mainly because I want to keep this on the down-low, but that's not the only reason. You've been in my office. You see a whole lot of bright bulbs in the chandelier?"

"Well…"

"And if there's no boyfriend in the woodpile, I just can't shake the feeling that she might just try and do it herself. Mix some rat poison in with his Raisin Bran, or find some miracle ingredient that'll give him a heart attack. None of which she could possibly get away with, not with her having established herself as a person of interest even before there's a case to be a person of interest *in*. That husband of hers dies of anything, any damn thing from galloping diarrhea to a flash flood, she'll be hearing her Miranda rights before the body gets to room temperature. Which is fine from our point of view, but it doesn't do a lot for George, does it?"

He'd finally mentioned a name. Not that anybody could have heard him, or made anything of it if they did.

"What keeps eating at me," Radburn went on, "is I can't shake the notion that I ought to have a talk with him."

"The husband."

"Uh-huh. What stops me is there's so many ways that can do more harm than good. 'Thanks for your concern, Sheriff, but I'm sure there's nothing to worry about.' Then he goes home and thinks it over, and loads his gun, and sits up waiting for her to come home from work."

"Jesus."

"So maybe she's the one I ought to be having that talk with. 'We know what you got in mind, and no matter how slick you are, no matter who actually does the deed, no matter what kind of alibi you've got for yourself, anything happens to him and we're on you like white on rice.'"

"And she says she doesn't know what the hell you're talking about."

"But she does know, and I know she knows, and she knows I know she knows. Believe me, it's not a conversation I want to have. But how's it look if he gets killed on my watch? Yes, I'll close the case, but it's my fault the man's dead."

Should he have seen this coming? Maybe, but what could he have done differently? And at least he was in on things, with a ringside seat.

"Don't say anything to anybody just yet," he said. "Let me see what I can find out for you."

EIGHTEEN

He held off checking his phone until he'd walked the sheriff back to his office, then returned to his car. Once again he'd left the windows all the way up, and he took it out on the highway and ran it at speed with the windows all the way down.

After a couple of miles it was cool enough for the air conditioner to hold its own. By then he was well out of town. He pulled into a rest area, got a Coke from the machine. There were tables and benches, but the county's site maintenance didn't extend to cleaning the birdshit off the furniture, so he drank the Coke standing up with his back against a tree.

He checked the Lisa phone, and there were no messages, nothing on his voicemail, no notification of missed calls. He'd told her not to call, and now he couldn't decide whether to be pleased or disappointed that she'd followed instructions.

On the other phone, there was voicemail from Barb. He played it: "Call me."

He did, and got her voicemail. "Tag," he said. "You're it."

He was taking the last swig of Coke when the phone rang. "Whew," she said. "What a morning! This couple from Michigan, looking for a condo they can use in the winter and rent out in the off-season, or maybe a time share, or maybe this or maybe that, so I've got a ton of things to show them, and not much chance of closing anything, because they don't know what they want. And you know how it always winds up, don't you? By the time they zero in on what they're really looking for, they've taken up so much of my time that they're embarrassed. So they don't call me, they call someone like that cunt Maggie Fitch, pardon my French, and she shows them one property and they offer the asking price, and where does that leave me?"

"High and dry?"

"At the moment," she said, "I'm neither one of those things. And hearing your voice is making me all wet."

"I've barely said a word. Is it safe to guess that you're behind closed doors?"

"Uh-huh. Touching myself very lightly through my panties, but I could probably be talked into taking them off."

"Why don't you come over?"

"You're home?"

"I could be," he said, "in ten minutes or so."

"You're not in the mood for conversation, is that what I'm hearing?"

"I think I'd like something a little more hands-on."

"Well, sugar, I already told you what my hand's on, and what your hand's on is strictly up to you."

"Just think how much better the conversation could be," he said, "with you touching yourself, same as you're doing now—"

"And?"

"And something in your ass."

"Something like what?"

"Something that's getting harder the more we talk about it."

She took a deep breath.

"Okay, we're on the same page," she said, "and it's got dirty words written all over it. I can't come now."

"Well, don't. Wait until we're together."

"I can't come *over* now. Unless I cancel an appointment, and I really don't want to do that. I could come by around four."

"Four would work."

"Four o'clock at your place."

✿

That was good, four o'clock. That gave him plenty of time to do some work for Gallatin County.

Though not necessarily the work the Sheriff expected him to be doing.

George Otterbein had turned over most of the day-to-day operations of Otterbein Kitchen Supply to his son, Alden. But he kept a suite of offices in Perry, on the second floor of a three-story red-brick building on Court House Square.

There was a café, Grounds for Divorce, two doors down from the court house and diagonally across the street from Otterbein's building. They had little glass-topped tables on the sidewalk, and Doak took one of them and ordered an iced mocha latte and a cranberry scone. It was, he thought, quite a step for Taylor County, where the greater portion of the population thought grits was one of the four basic food groups.

A phone call earlier had established that Otterbein had gone to lunch, and Doak kept an eye on the entrance.

"Mr. O's usually back around one," the woman had said, "but I wouldn't swear it'll be like that today."

"I guess you can't set your watch by him."

"Well, no," she said. "Now that you put it that way, no, I'd have to say you can't."

But at five minutes before one, he recognized the man he'd seen in online photos. The face was unmistakable—a big beak of a nose, a jutting chin, overgrown eyebrows—and Otterbein was taller and heavier than his pictures had suggested, dwarfing the younger man walking at his side.

Otterbein clapped his companion on the shoulder, then parted company with him to disappear into the red-brick building. Doak settled his check, walked to his car. He'd left a seersucker jacket folded over the passenger seat. Otterbein had been wearing a suit, so he donned the jacket; Otterbein's shirt had been open, so he left his own necktie in his jacket pocket.

"J. W. Miller for Mr. Otterbein," he said, handing over a card. "I called earlier."

He took a seat while the woman who couldn't set her clock by her employer took him Doak's card, coming back shortly to say Mr. Otterbein would see him. He found Otterbein standing in shirtsleeves behind a massive oak desk, his jacket hanging on a walnut hat tree in the corner.

"Mr. Miller," Otterbein said. "Marcie didn't say what this is in reference to, but I don't suppose she asked you, did she?"

"I don't believe so."

"She never does. I think she's afraid of invading your privacy, but I'm not." He squinted at the card. "Inquiries, it says here. What's that mean?"

"It means I wanted one card that would cover all the bases," he said. "I'm a retired police officer from up North, getting along just fine without the cold weather. A little work now and then stretches my pension some and keeps me from rusting out."

And why did that bring him to Otterbein's office?

"I might have a few dollars for you," he said. "If you're the right Otterbein."

Back home on Osprey Drive, he hung the seersucker jacket in the closet, took another shower. He started to get dressed, then changed his mind and put on a robe.

He found things to do on the computer, and around three-thirty he took a call from Barb. Were they still on for four?

He said they were, and a few minutes before the hour he

heard her car make the turn into his drive. He was at the door when she reached it, and she met him with an open-mouthed kiss and a hand reaching into his robe.

"God, what a day," she said. "But you're gonna make me forget all about it, aren't you?"

NINETEEN

At ten-thirty the next morning he was parked near the entrance to the Cinema Village fourplex at the Chiefland Mall. He didn't have to wait long before the silver Lexus pulled alongside.

"The screens are dark until noon," he told her. "We're better off leaving your car at the other end, over by the Penney's. Go find a spot and I'll pick you up."

She nodded and parked among the mall's few dozen customers, and when she joined him in the Monte Carlo he must have been staring, because she asked what was wrong.

He said, "I forget how beautiful you are."

"Oh, please."

"It's your eyes, I think. The blue of them. It's always more intense than I remember."

"Do we really have a love nest? Or was that just a story?"

In bed she said, "So? Who'd you get? The pregnant lady?"

Roberta Ellison, née Bobbie Jondahl.

"The other one," he said.

"Real Estate Girl. What's her name?"

"Barbara Hamill."

"Do I know her? I don't think so. Is she a Barbie Doll, all tits and a tiny waist?"

"She goes by Barb, and her waist's a ways from tiny."

"Is she a fatty? Do you get to wallow around in all that flesh?"

"She's not fat."

"Nice tits?"

"They're okay," he said. "Her ass is her best feature."

"Nicer than mine?"

"There's no part of anybody that's nicer than any part of you."

"Yeah, right. But Barbie's got a great ass? Pardon me, I mean Barb. Does she make the most of it? Does she like it in the ass?"

"She does now."

"She didn't but now she does? Thanks to kindly old Doctor Miller?"

He told her about the phone sex, the tranny fantasy. "Yesterday," he said, "we had some more phone sex. But without the phone."

"Tell me about the couple."

"What couple? Oh, those two time-wasters with no idea what they wanted? There's nothing to tell."

"Make something up."

"What do you mean? They weren't hot enough to have a fantasy about."

"So make them hotter. Make her beautiful, make him handsome."

"And?"

"You're showing this house, and they put the moves on you."

"Not those two, but okay, I get it. Give me a minute, let me think, and how am I supposed to think with you inside me? Oh, Jesus. Well, you're right, she's a beauty, in a sort of unformed girlish kind of way. And he's not handsome, in fact you'd have to say he was ugly, but like a dangerous bad guy in a movie, you know? Very sexy, you're scared of him but there's something about him that makes you want to fuck him."

"And?"

"And right away I got a little bit of a tingle from the way he

looked, and the way he was looking at me. And I got the feeling
he wanted to make a move, but how could he with his wife there?

"So I'm showing them this palatial condo, top floor with a
storybook view, and I know it's out of their price range but I
take them there anyway, and he goes to use the bathroom, and
the wife comes up and slips her arm around my waist, and in
the most matter-of-fact way she says, 'You know, Barb, my husband would totally love to fuck you.'"

"So the move came from her."

"And I swear I never saw it coming! There she is with her
hand on my hip, and she moves it so she's stroking my ass, real
gently, yes, like you're doing now, that's right—"

"And?"

"And she says, 'And I'd like to watch him, I'd like to see his
big hard cock going in and out of you, and after he fills you full
of cum I'll get down there and clean you up and make you come
all over again.'"

"You must have been excited."

"Crazy excited, and scared at the same time, because I never
did anything like this, I was never with a woman and certainly
never with a couple and—oh, I wish you would fuck me hard,
but you're just going to keep it inside me, aren't you, and not
move at all, and, and—"

"Did they do what she said?"

"He fucked me really hard. Held my legs up over my head so
he could get in really deep, and it hurt me some but I was too
hot to care. And she was kissing me all over my face and pinching
my nipples, pinching them really hard, and I generally don't like
that, but this time it seemed right. And talking to me while she's
kissing me, all this breathy love talk, 'Oh, you're so pretty, you're
so sweet.' And his cock, hammering away at me, and I came so
hard I just about blacked out.

"And the next thing I knew, she had her face between my legs and she was licking my pussy and I knew I wasn't going to respond because I'd just come so hard. But I thought, well, pay attention, because this is a new experience for you and you might as well see what it's like. And it was different, you know, a woman's mouth is different, and knowing it's a woman doing it, that makes it different, too. And before I knew it I was excited all over again, and not just a little excited but really crazy hot, and I started to come, and she kept eating me and I just kept coming.

"And I'm lying there, and he's holding my head, turning it so my face is right in front of her pussy. And he's like, 'Time to return the favor, don't you think?' And she's all, 'No, Barb, only if you want to,' and it hits me that I have to taste her, that I'll die if I don't get my mouth on her. And it's not like I don't know what girls taste like, I've touched myself and sucked my finger a million times, but now I'm licking her and it's amazing, and then I feel him behind me, and he's fucking me while I'm eating out his beautiful wife, and—"

"And it never happened," Lisa said. "She just made it up."

"Right."

"I'd say Scheherazade gets to live another night. And you were doing her while she was telling you the story."

"Uh-huh. It's not word for word, but it's as close as I could come without taping her."

"That might be interesting."

"What, taping her?"

"Be easy enough, right there in your own house. Then we could actually hear her telling the story. Or is it better with you recounting it to me? Hmmm."

"Hmmm indeed."

"And you were inside her while she was talking? Like you're inside me now?"

"Well, I was in her—"

"Ass, right. Barb's best feature. Do you want to be in my ass? So we can replicate the experience?"

"I don't want to move from where I am."

"Then stay right where you are. I could come like this. Could you?"

"Uh-huh."

"But I don't think I want to, not right now. Is that weird?"

"I feel the same way."

"Like coming is nice, but it's sort of beside the point. You know what I like about our love nest?"

"The smell of stale cigarette smoke."

"Which is something you generally miss out on in a non-smoking room. Though right now the smell of sex is doing a good job of canceling it out. No, what I was going to say is that I'm glad the place is tacky."

"So you can get to feel lowdown and dirty?"

"No," she said. "I could feel like that in a palace. No, but imagine if we had a really nice place. And we could, you know. There are a million condos for rent, time shares people can't give away, and how hard could it be to arrange everything through a third party and keep it all nicely anonymous? We could lie on percale sheets while we were grooving on your girlfriend's naughty stories."

"Now I'm beginning to regret bringing you to a dump like this."

"No, that's the whole point. If we had a place like that we could stay there forever."

He thought about it. "Oh," he said.

"Do you see what I mean? It would be comfortable. I don't want us to be comfortable."

"I get it," he said. "And you're right. And here's something to keep you from getting too comfortable."

"Am I gonna like this?"

"I don't know," he said. "I took a ride over to Court House Square earlier today. I went and had a talk with your husband, George."

It was something he'd thought of doing, he told her, but it was the conversation with the sheriff that had changed the thought to action. He had to get more of a sense of the man than you could get by stalking him online. And it made sense to establish himself in George's eyes, so that when he turned up down the line he was already a known factor, that New York cop scraping by doing odd jobs for lawyers and insurance agents. Miller, his name was, a forgettable name with a couple of forgettable initials to keep it company, and he was certainly nobody to take seriously, nobody to worry about.

There might be some money, he'd told the man. If you're the right Otterbein.

Which, of course, George had proved not to be.

The legend Doak spun was simple enough. A childless widower in Scottsbluff, Nebraska, had died at an advanced age. The old gentleman, one Elmer Otterbein, had never left the family farm, but he'd worked hard and saved himself rich. Well, seven figures worth of rich. He'd died intestate with a few million in savings and government bonds and acreage worth about as much. There was, in short, enough money involved to spend a small fraction of it looking for legitimate heirs, before it disappeared into the coffers of the great state of Nebraska.

And Otterbein, while by no means a common name, was hardly unique. Two Midwestern cities bore the name, as did the college in Ohio and a residential neighborhood in Baltimore. So if George Otterbein could establish any connection to Otterbeins in Nebraska or South Dakota—

"It bothered him that he couldn't," he told Lisa. "He really wanted to be the missing heir, but his father was born right here in Florida to a family with all its connection in Maryland and Virginia. Then he managed to recall a sister of his grandfather's who'd married a man and moved west, and when I pointed out that a sister wouldn't have been able to pass on the Otterbein name, he decided that it might as easily have been a brother. I took down his information and we agreed that it was unlikely to lead anywhere, but there was no harm in seeing where it went."

"God, that's George. If there's a nickel looking for a home, he'll be happy to take it in. He told me once he's not related to any of the Otterbeins, that his father was the only son of an only son. Of course that was when a young man named Otterbein applied for a job, and went so far as to suggest that they might be related. George didn't encourage the speculation, nor did he hire the fellow, who he thought was looking to con him."

"He had the same thought about me."

"Oh?"

"He'd had a drink or two with lunch, and he took down a bottle and poured himself another. Talked me into joining him, either to be sociable or to loosen me up. I think he was waiting for me to offer to work up some credentials to support his claim. A lot of short cons play off that sort of premise, and most of them wind up asking for some kind of expense money, with the real payoff to come when the legacy comes in."

"Which it never does."

"The front money *is* the payoff, for the con man. And you'd think that'd be it, that he'd take it and disappear, but sometimes a good player can string a mark along for months. Getting an extra hundred here and there, a few bucks to underwrite a search of Cree tribal records in Manitoba, a few bucks more to bribe a vital statistics clerk in Mandan, North Dakota."

"But you didn't ask him for money."

"Of course not. I got a few minutes of his time and an ounce or two of his single-malt scotch, and that was really all I wanted. More than I wanted, because I've never been much of a scotch drinker, and it was a little early in the day for me anyway. How old is George? I read it online and it didn't stick. Well up in his sixties, gotta be."

"Sixty-seven this past March."

"He still looks vigorous, but I guess there's no reason a man his age wouldn't be."

"Are we talking about sexual potency here? Because he can still get it up, if that was the question."

"It wasn't. He's big and he looks strong. The drink shows in his face a little. Does he get any exercise?"

"He plays golf, but I don't know if that counts as exercise. They all use carts, and how much exercise is it to swing a club a few dozen times?"

"They really don't walk?"

"On some courses you're not allowed to. You have to use a cart, because otherwise it slows things down too much."

"I never played," he said, "but I always thought the one good thing about it would be all that walking in the open air. I've seen them playing golf on TV, the different tournaments. I don't remember them zipping around in carts."

"Maybe it's different on TV."

"Maybe. You were going to tell me what made you cut your hair."

"Right."

"It doesn't have to be now. If you'd rather wait—"

"No," she said. "Now's a good time for it. Especially now that you went and saw him. And had a drink with him. Speaking of which, you didn't happen to bring any whiskey along, did you?"

"It never occurred to me. I could go get some, though I don't know offhand where the nearest package store would be, but—"

"No, don't go anywhere. If our love nest happened to have a stocked bar, I'd be a customer. But I'm probably better off without it. I've never told anybody this story, but then I've never told anybody anything, not really. Until I met you."

He waited.

"I said I'd need you to hold me. Not now. You'll know when."

TWENTY

"The problem was I didn't get pregnant. If I had his baby it would prove something. Don't ask me what, but it was very important to him. And we tried and tried and tried, and we went to a fertility doctor and had tests done, and it just didn't happen.

"His kids hated me before they even met me. I already told you that. They thought I was just interested in him for his money, and they weren't entirely wrong about that. I was impressed with him, he's a big powerful man and he has an aura, you know? A magnetism, even.

"But his money was a big factor. I always worked and I always got by, but I was getting tired of the struggle. It was this constant struggle. I was always sweating the rent or the car payment, always a day late and a dollar short.

"And here was this man who wanted to take care of me. He had plenty of money, he'd made something for himself on top of what his daddy left him, and his kids were grown and he wanted someone to take care of, someone to spoil.

"So I looked at what cards I was holding and I played them carefully. I wouldn't fuck him because I was just scared to death of getting pregnant, that's what I told him, which turned out to be ironic when my period showed up right on time every month. Instead I would give him hand jobs, until I let him talk me into using my mouth. I had to act like I didn't know what I was doing, and bit by bit little miss virgin mouth figured out what to do, and even learned to like it.

"Maybe I should have been an actress.

"So he married me, and I finally let him put it in, and I think what ruined it all for me was the acting. I was never in love with him, but I think maybe I could have come to love him if I hadn't sabotaged it. But when you play somebody that way you wind up having contempt for him, because he'd have to be a moron to buy your act. And because the number you're doing on him is only justified if you tell yourself he's an asshole and he deserves it.

"Anyway, it was okay on the surface for a while. I learned how to shop, and that was fun until it wasn't, until the novelty wore off. Some women get addicted, they can spend their whole lives shopping, but it didn't do much for me once I got the hang of it.

"I got tired of it. We got tired of each other. Trying to get pregnant was part of it. Having to do it on schedule, and in positions that were supposed to facilitate conception, that turned it into a job. And it *was* my job, you know, except I'd been trying to avoid facing up to the fact.

"Then we quit trying, and I was tired of his dick and he was tired of my pussy. And I thought, okay, the honeymoon's over, and maybe that's all right. I can still be a wife. I can run the house, I can show up with him at social functions and look good on his arm, I can remember the names of his friends and flirt just enough to make them want me but not enough so that they think they've got a chance.

"I thought we were okay. And in the long run, well, he was thirty years older, wasn't he? More than that, he was exactly twice my age when we got married, sixty-two to my thirty-one, and he wasn't a drunk but he was a man who drank, and you probably noticed the bloom on his nose and cheeks, the broken blood vessels. His daddy taught him to drink Kentucky bourbon, and he switched to single-malt scotch when someone let him know that was classier, and he didn't get drunk but he pretty much always had a drink in him, and according to the charts the insurance men show you, he was thirty pounds overweight. He carries it well, but it's there, isn't it?

"So how long could he expect to live? Eighty years is a lot and seventy-five's probably more like it, and when he's seventy-five I'll be forty-four, and I won't get everything or even close to it, but the pre-nup that's got me locked in, it locks him in, too. He can't give it all to the kids. They get most of it, but I get the house, and I get the insurance money, and I get—well, I wind up okay.

"So I'm letting myself get used to it, this life I'm living, and he's drinking more than usual. Which is a bad thing when he gets ugly drunk and talks mean to me but a good thing when he goes to bed right after he's had his dinner.

"Then one night he brings a man home with him.

"A younger man, one of those Mexicans who queue up every morning at the turnoff in Perry, looking for day labor. 'This is Nando,' he says. 'He's gonna fuck you.'

"I told him he was drunk and crazy, and I told Nando to get the hell out of my house, but they didn't pay any attention to me. I figured out later that he'd explained to Nando that I'd be playing a part, that I'd pretend to fight, and that what I really wanted was to be forced. And that's what happened. Nando raped me.

"He hit me. I don't think he wanted to, I don't think violence toward women came naturally to him, but George was there urging him on. 'Go ahead, slap her! That's what the bitch wants, that's what gets her motor running. Give her a good one!'

"I don't know what would have happened if I fought back. Maybe they would have stopped. But I just went numb.

"George made him wear a condom. If he couldn't get me pregnant he didn't want some Mexican doing it. It may have been Nando's first time with his dick wrapped.

"So we're in bed and Nando's on top of me. And, you know, inside of me. And I've got my eyes closed and I'm just waiting for it to be over.

"And smelling him. Nando. I suppose personal hygiene is hard to prioritize when you're a day laborer sharing a shack on the highway with eight or ten other men, sleeping in shifts on sheets that never get washed. And living on chili and garlic, stuff that comes out of your pores, and if you're not able to bathe regularly, it builds up.

"And at one point I open my eyes, and George is on a chair pulled up next to the bed, and his pants are down and he's got his dick in one hand and a gun in the other. He owns a lot of guns and he keeps one in the drawer of the bedside table and that's the one he's got now, a little pistol, blued steel with swirly green grips. Malachite, that's what they were.

"And I know somebody's gonna get killed, me or Nando or both of us. 'Sheriff, I caught them together and I did what I had to do.'

"Well, nobody got shot. He never did put the gun down, it stayed in his left hand, but he gathered up a fistful of my long hair in his right hand and wrapped it around his cock. And he jerked himself off with my hair.

"Nando finished, he cried out and grunted and rolled off of me, and George let out a matching grunt and came in my hair. He kept right on pumping so that I wouldn't miss a drop, and then he took my hair and rubbed it all over my face. Didn't say a word, just walked out of the room.

"The first thing I did was douche, and then I must have spent two hours under the shower. I used a whole bottle of shampoo, I washed everything.

"You'd better hold me now. Yes, like that. That's good.

"When I was through, when I was out of the shower and

dried off, the bedroom was empty. At first I thought I was alone in the house. There's a live-in maid, but her room's on the third floor and she disappears into it as soon as she's done with the after-dinner cleanup. You never hear a peep out of her.

"I went downstairs and found George passed out on the living room sofa. He was fully dressed except for his shoes. They were on the floor next to him.

"I guess he must have given Nando a ride somewhere. Or just handed him a fistful of twenties and shoved him out the door. I'm sure he paid him. 'Here, fuck my wife, I'll make it worth your while.'

"I patted his pockets, looking for the gun. I found it upstairs in the bedroom in the nightstand drawer where he kept it. I'd never actually touched it before, guns make me nervous, but I picked it up and held it in my hand. It's a small gun, I don't know the caliber, but it was the right size for my hand. And the malachite grips were cool to the touch, and perfectly smooth.

"I went back downstairs. He hadn't moved, he was lying on his back with his mouth half-open.

"I held the gun to his temple, then to his forehead. I let the metal touch his skin, I pressed it so that it left an impression when I took it away, a little round O in the middle of his forehead.

"That was the size of the hole it would make if I pulled the trigger.

"I'd say I thought about it, but I don't remember any thoughts.

"I went upstairs. I put the gun back in the drawer. I stripped the bed and made it up with fresh sheets and pillowcases.

"In the morning I went to my hairdresser and told him he had to fit me in. When I let him know what I wanted he kept asking me if I was sure. 'Lisa, girlfriend, don't you want to think this over?' He was afraid to do it, but I told him if he didn't cut it I'd cut it myself. Well, he couldn't let that happen, so he cut it, and I kept saying, 'No, shorter,' and he cut it the way it is today. I've kept it like this ever since.

"I drove straight from the beauty parlor to the Cattle Baron, and when I left there I had my old job back. I lucked out, the hostess had given notice and he needed to find somebody to replace her, but I think I'd have gotten the job anyway, even if he had to fire somebody. He always liked me.

"I went home. The maid gaped when she saw my hair. George was out, and it was dark out by the time he came home. He'd been drinking but he wasn't drunk. He looked at me and his face didn't change expression.

"I told him I'd be going to work, that I had my old job back. He just nodded.

"We never said anything about the previous evening. He never brought anybody home again. And about a month later we were in bed, and he started touching me. I didn't stop him. And then he got on top of me, and I went along with it.

"The little gun's still in the nightstand drawer. Sometimes I open the drawer and look at it, but I never pick it up, or even touch it."

He went out, drove around, bought pizza and brought it back to the room. They ate the pizza and drank Cokes from the machine and she apologized for ruining the mood. He told her not to be ridiculous.

She said, "Your stories get us hot. Then I tell a story and turn us off completely. I never told that story before. Maybe I should have taken it to the grave."

"I'm glad you told me."

"And I'm glad I told you, but look at the mood it's put us in. Here we are in our love nest, and it's wasted on us. You're shaking your head."

"Because it's not wasted. What did you just call it?"

"Call what? This place? I called it our love nest, but that's how you've been referring to it since you paid the rent."

"Because that's what it is."

"I don't—"

"Not our fuck nest," he said. "Our love nest."

"Oh."

"And I love you."

She was holding a slice of pizza, and now she looked at it as if couldn't remember what she was supposed to do with it. She put it down and turned her blue eyes to him.

She said, "We've never said that, have we? I've been calling you darling, which is fairly extreme all by itself, but we've stayed away from the L word."

"It's been in my mind."

"And mine."

"I tell you everything else. I ought to be able to tell you I love you."

"And I love you."

"And your story got us here, so stop apologizing for it."

"All right."

"I love your hair this way. It shows off your face, it makes your blue eyes big enough to drown in."

"I was wondering if you might like me better with long hair."

"No, keep it this way."

"I will."

"And your story serves a practical purpose, too."

"Oh?"

"It'll make it a whole lot easier," he said, "when the time comes to kill him."

TWENTY-ONE

He dropped her at the Chiefland Mall. She headed north in the Lexus, on her way to work, and he thought about a movie, but the four films on offer were aimed at a much younger audience. The films he liked were to be found on cable channels.

He drove home, checked his email, had a shower, drank a beer, watched a couple of Eastern European women play tennis. They were both blonde, they were both wearing white, and neither one had a name he could pronounce, so he found them essentially indistinguishable. He watched without really paying attention, hit the Mute button to shut up the announcers, then found he missed the sound of the bouncing ball. He took it off Mute and just ignored what they were saying.

And after the sun was down he found himself watching a movie, *Double Indemnity* on TCM. He'd recalled it a few days ago, while he was doing the job for Newhouser, and when channel-surfing brought it to his attention, he could hardly pass it up.

Barbara Stanwyck and—for God's sake, Fred MacMurray, acting in what had to be the only dark role of his career, and playing the hell out of it. He was an insurance agent and she was married to a policy holder and they hatched a plot to kill her husband for the insurance. And there was Edward G. Robinson, on the side of the angels for a change, playing the tough claims investigator who wouldn't let them get away with it.

All in black and white, which suited the film's classic noir mood, and TCM showed it without commercials, and he started out appreciating it and wound up caught up entirely in the story. He had to go to the bathroom, his bladder was stretched to capacity, but he waited until the final credits had rolled before he got up from his chair.

The subject matter, of course, may have had something to do with it.

They were going to have to kill George Otterbein.

No way around it, really. The pre-nuptial agreement he'd had her sign had been drawn by one of the state's foremost matrimonial lawyers. It defined her participation in her husband's estate, specifying just how much and how little he could leave her. If he were to divorce her, it set the terms of the divorce settlement in advance. She'd get something along the lines of a half million dollars. That was certainly a substantial sum, but far less than she might otherwise have expected to receive.

On the other hand, if she were the one to institute divorce proceedings, or if she physically ceased cohabitation with him, she'd be cut off with fifty thousand dollars.

That was more money than she'd brought to the marriage, when her net worth had consisted of the clothes in her closet and her equity in the eight-year-old car she was driving. But it was roughly a tenth of what he'd have to pay her if he was the one who wanted the divorce, and the difference was enough to explain why he was comfortable sharing his bed and board with a woman who'd come to despise him. And it pretty much guaranteed that life with George was not going to get better for her, because he had every reason—well, every reason with a dollar sign in front of it—to make her unhappy enough to walk out.

Fifty thousand dollars. You could see all the options just by moving the decimal point around. Half a million if George got the divorce. Something in the neighborhood of five million if he died.

Sunday he spent most of the morning online. Around noon he got in the car, stopped at an ATM, then drove for a little over an hour to Quitman, Georgia. He filled the tank at a BP station and got directions to the local high school, where they were holding a gun and knife show. It seemed an unfortunate venue, with school shootings so frequently in the news, but maybe the local school board missed the memo.

He parked in the high school lot, where his Monte Carlo looked at home among a good batch of clunkers, and followed the signs to the school gymnasium. Some two dozen dealers had their wares displayed on folding aluminum tables, and at least that many prospective customers were looking at what was on offer.

He found the edged weapons more interesting than the guns. Most of the tables showed at least a few of them, and they were a specialty of one dealer, whose stock included everything from a Civil War cavalry saber and Nazi daggers to army surplus combat knives and bench-made hunters and folders.

Years ago he'd carried a pocket knife, but after it disappeared he'd replaced it with a Swiss Army knife. The replacement was wonderfully handy, it boasted a blade for every contingency, but the thing was too bulky to carry in your pocket, and his stayed on his desk. He thought he might like to have one of these custom-made folding knives, and checked out a few of them, noting the features that enabled them to be opened one-handed, and the various locking mechanisms that kept a blade from snapping shut on your thumb in the middle of a task.

Very nice, and it would handy to carry a pocket knife once

again. He spent fifteen minutes narrowing his selection down to two specimens, and by then he decided he was just wasting his time, because he didn't plan to stab George Otterbein, or slash his throat, and if he did he'd do okay with a ten-dollar chef's knife from Walmart.

He drove back across the Florida state line with a revolver and a pistol and a box of shells for each.

"This here's your Taurus Ultra-Lite," said the bearded man who sold him the revolver. "Got your rubber grips, your stainless steel finish. Shoots the .32 H&R Magnum round. Six shots, two-inch barrel, goes in your pocket or her purse, don't weigh you down, and you've got enough stopping power for most tasks."

"I guess you know what you're lookin' at," said the clean-shaven man who sold him the pistol. "That's a Ruger, an' of course it's a niner, comes with a ten-shot clip. Be a pricey gun if you was to buy it new, and it's not that far from new condition, as you can see. You sure you don't want to add on a second clip? Saves having to reload when you're, um, pressed for time."

Back home, he looked for a place to stow the guns and ammo. He already owned one gun, a five-shot Smith & Wesson revolver that had come with a full box of .38 Special cartridges. Not long after he'd closed on the house, he'd bought the gun over the counter at a local sporting goods store. Paid for it with his Visa card, showed the requisite ID, signed his real name to the register.

That gun was in his nightstand drawer; the box of shells, full but for the five he'd loaded into the Smith, was on a shelf in the closet. He'd never fired it, not even to test it. He didn't see that he needed to get the hang of it, as it wasn't that different from the service revolver he'd carried on the job in New York.

And the last time he'd fired that particular gun, somebody had died.

At the same time that he'd bought the Smith, he'd picked up a gun cleaning kit, with solvent and oil and brushes and cleaning patches. It was on the same closet shelf as the box of .38 Special shells. He'd never opened it, but now he unfastened the canvas roll-up pouch and spent half an hour cleaning the two weapons he'd just purchased. They both looked clean enough to him, spotless in fact, but he'd bought these for actual use, not to sit in a drawer, and it seemed no more than prudent to make sure they were as close to immaculate as he could make them.

And the task itself was pleasantly mechanical. It gave his mind a chance to wander.

He hadn't signed anything for the Taurus or the Ruger. The bearded fellow never even raised the subject, just conducted the transaction with no more ceremony than if Doak had been purchasing a can of window putty. The man with the Ruger had flashed him a conspiratorial look and said, "Now of course you've been a legal resident of the state of Georgia for no less than thirty days. Goes without sayin', don't it?" He didn't wait for a nod. "And you've never been convicted of a felony, or spent any time in a mental institution, nor do you have any intent to commit a crime, harm another human being, or overthrow the lawful government of either the state of Georgia or the United States of America. We good with that?"

Cleaning the guns let him get used to them, their weight, the way they felt in his hand.

But where to keep them? Technically, their possession entailed a certain risk, in that they were unregistered handguns, but he wouldn't have cared to guess at the percentage of Gallatin County households in the same position. From a practical standpoint, the guns posed no danger to him until he put them to their intended use.

Of course, he thought, their provenance was unknown to him. They'd come into his possession with no paper trail, he hadn't requested or been offered a receipt for either transaction, and who was to say that a previous owner hadn't used the Taurus in a holdup, or reached for the Ruger when an episode of road rage got out of hand?

Don't put that gun in your mouth, son. You don't know where it's been.

Where he kept the guns was not hugely important, but working it out saved him from thinking about other more difficult questions. So he devoted more time to the matter than it probably required.

He ruled out the nightstand, where he kept the Smith, and the closet shelf that held the Smith's spare ammo. Ditto the garage, where the most casual sort of prowler could walk off with them.

He'd never bought a safe, didn't own anything that required that sort of protection. And the trouble with a safe was that it was the first and most obvious place for a person to look. Most of the time the person in question was a burglar who'd spin the combination dial twice and give up, but he was more worried about someone with a badge who could point to the safe and ask him to open it.

Easy enough to pry a baseboard loose and create a hiding place behind it, but wasn't that likely to be more trouble than it was worth? It would take time to do, and so would retrieving the guns when he wanted them.

Nor would it stand up to a thorough search, and that was the sort that most concerned him. He'd been a part of enough efforts of that nature—looking for dealers' drug stashes, more often than not—to know how many ways there were to hide something, and how futile most of them ultimately proved to be.

Hard to play innocent, too, when a couple of cops with x-ray vision move your dresser aside, pull up your carpet, pry a few floorboards loose, and find what you'd concealed there. *Oh, that thing, Officer? Just a safety precaution. I didn't want to leave it out where the neighbor's kid might play with it.*

He wound up tucking everything into a kitchen cupboard. The kitchenware he'd bought didn't amount to much, and fit with room left over into those cupboards within easy reach. There was a top tier of cupboards, and to get into the one at the far left you had to either stand on a chair or play in the NBA. He'd stood on a chair once, to assure himself it was empty; he did so again now, and when he got down from the chair, his gun show purchases had a new home.

TWENTY-TWO

In the morning he checked for a message from Lisa, called her when he didn't find one. His call went straight to voicemail, and it was several hours before she got back to him.

"Today's a mess," she said. "Can we meet tomorrow?" And, after they'd set a time, "Gotta go. Bye."

He set the phone down with a sense that something was wrong. The brevity of the conversation, her hurry to be done with it—

The phone rang. He picked it up and said, "Can you talk now?" but it went on ringing, and he realized it was the other phone.

Caller ID showed a number he recognized but couldn't place. He took the call, said "Miller."

A woman said, "Mr. Miller? Will you hold for Mr. Otterbein?"

Really?

He said he would, and a moment later Otterbein was on the line. "Miller," he said. "You find any more of my long-lost relatives?"

"I'm afraid I've stopped looking," he said. "Unless you've remembered something you think might prove useful."

"I haven't, and as much as I'd like to embrace Cousin Elmer— did I get that right? Elmer?"

"Elmer Otterbein."

"Nice to know I can remember his name, even if I can't come up with a way for us to be blood kin. You swamped with work, Miller?"

"I beg your pardon?"

"You got a deskful of missing heirs and such? Because you've been on my mind ever since you walked into my office."

"Oh?"

"So why don't you walk into it a second time," he said, "and we'll talk. You found your way here the once so you shouldn't have any trouble finding it again. Say half an hour?"

At eleven-thirty the following morning he pulled into the Chiefland Mall. The Lexus was already there, at the J. C. Penney side of the lot. He drove them to their motel, and in the car she said she'd been more abrupt than she intended the last time they'd talked. But she'd been rushed, she explained, and an earlier exchange with George had left her short-tempered.

In their room, with the doughnut on the outside doorknob and the bolt turned, she came into his arms and kissed him, and something relaxed within both of them, some knot of tension dissolved and went away.

When the embrace ended they stood a few feet apart on the worn carpet and took off all their clothes. His heart filled at the sight of her.

And not just his heart. "Look at you," she said, and reached to take hold of him. "Oh, no stories today, no drama, nothing. Just fuck me."

Afterward he said, "Story time. I'm afraid it's not a bedtime story, because I've been going to bed alone since the last time we were in this little room. But I saw your husband again."

"Was that wise?"

"Well, it was that or hang up on him. He called me."

He told her about the call, and about the meeting forty minutes later in Otterbein's office. "He gave me a card with a name and address on it," he said, "and showed me a woman's picture."

"I hope I was wearing more in the picture than I am now."

"It wasn't you," he said. "George has a girlfriend."

Her name, he said, was Ashley Hannon, and she had recently moved into a side-by-side duplex on Stapleton Terrace. She was twenty-seven years old, with a General Studies diploma from a two-year college in Ocala and a certificate from the Broward County Physiotherapy Institute attesting to her competence in Shiatsu, Swedish massage, and Reiki, and there was something else, but he couldn't remember what it was.

"Fellatio," Lisa suggested.

"That may have come under General Studies. She spent two years in Broward County, mostly in Pompano Beach, and then she moved to the Gulf Coast and took a position in a massage parlor in Clearwater."

"A position? Kneeling, would be my guess."

It wasn't a whorehouse, he told her. All of the women had undergone genuine massage training, with certificates similar to Ashley's. They used professional massage tables and offered a variety of techniques, and all you got for the posted rate was a standard non-sexual massage.

Anything beyond that was by arrangement with the technician.

"In other words," she said, "a Happy Ending. And just how happy it is depends on how much you pay. And then Clearwater must have had an Unhappy Ending for her to come to this backwater garden spot. How'd she wind up here, and how did George find her?"

"He found her in Clearwater."

"And brought her here? I suppose he's paying her rent."

"There's no rent to pay. He owns the building. The other half's rented to a black family with a couple of young kids."

"And Ashley's in the other half? Is she black?"

"White," he said. "Your basic cheerleader type with a head of blonde curls."

"I knew he liked professional talent," she said. "He never minded saying so, even when things were good between us. He showed me something he wanted me to do."

"What?"

"It's easier if I show you," she said. "Two fingers at the rear of your sack, and then like so. I think it has something to do with the prostate."

"I can see why he liked it."

"Oh? Well, there's no reason I can't haul it out of my own personal bag of tricks next time, if you're not bothered by knowing where it came from. I didn't ask George where it came from, but he told me anyway. He said very matter-of-factly that a girl in a massage parlor did it to him. I said I hoped he gave her a good tip. But he gave this one more than a tip, he gave her a house. When did she move in?"

"Six weeks ago."

"There would have had to be a whole string of Happy Endings first, wouldn't you think? When did he first stretch out on her massage table?"

"He didn't say, just that he'd met her in Clearwater and taken an interest."

"He didn't say what she was doing there?"

He shook his head. "You can find out a lot about a person online," he said. "If you know where to look, and what to look for. Her education and certification are a matter of record, and—"

"Have you seen her yet?"

"Just the photo, and no, I don't have it with me. He gave me a good look at it and then slipped it into a desk drawer. I drove past the house."

"You drove past mine, too. I bet hers isn't as nice."

"CBS," he said, "and that still sounds like the TV network, even though I've lived down here long enough to use the expression myself. Concrete block and stucco, two stories with a crawl-space attic. I think I said it's a side-by-side duplex. The other tenants have a swing-and-slide combo set up on the front lawn."

"I think I like our love nest better."

"I have the feeling he's thinking about moving her someplace a little more upscale."

"Someplace like Rumsey Road?"

"I don't know," he said. "He wants a background report on her, and he wants me to focus on her family. Her parents are both dead, and I guess she was a little vague about what they died of."

"He can't think she killed them. Oh, Jesus Christ. He's thinking about hereditary illnesses."

"That would be my guess."

"He's checking her out to find out what kind of a brood mare she'll make." She sat up, alarm showing on her face. "I wondered how she got him to move her up from Clearwater. I'm sure the girl's well-schooled, and in more than Shiatsu and Reiki—"

"Don't forget Swedish."

"—and I'm willing to believe she can suck a tennis ball through a garden hose, but all that would do is get him to drive down to Clearwater when the urge came on him. He wants to get her pregnant."

"It sounds like it."

"If she passes the background check, the next test is can he knock her up. When he got tested they told him there was nothing wrong with his sperm, and they didn't find anything wrong with me, either, and one doctor told me there seemed to be some way my uterus was rejecting his sperm. I have to say that makes me really proud of my uterus. It's clearly the most intelligent part of my body."

"If he gets her pregnant—"

"Oh, he will. Love will find a way. And if that happens, he'll want to marry her. No kid of his is going to grow up sharing a CBS duplex with a passel of pickaninnies."

"There's a word you don't hear much anymore."

"And that may be the first time it ever passed my lips. Darling, this could be good for us."

"Well, he'll pay me a nice fee for running a check on her, but beyond that—"

"He'll need a divorce from me before he can marry her."

"Unless he moves to Utah."

"And he can divorce me, but not without writing out a check for half a million dollars. I told you the terms of the pre-nup, right?"

"You did."

"That sounds like a fortune, half a million dollars. It's not, not really, not anymore, but it's a whole lot more than I had in my jeans when I said goodbye to the Twin Cities." She took a deep breath, let it out. "And it's not as though I've got any say in the matter. If he wants to divorce me that's what he'll do. Suppose we invest the money. What kind of income would I get?"

"I'm not the best person to answer that," he said, "but I can tell you this much. You'd be better off by a factor of ten if he died before he had a chance to divorce you."

"If he died," she said. "You mean if we killed him."

"I mean when we kill him."

"God," she said. She looked down at her folded hands, then up at him. "I know you're serious about it," she said, "but it's hard for me to know how serious. I mean, look at me. I was so stupid, making half-assed arrangements with Gonson. What saved me was when you showed up."

"With my fancy car."

"It did look like something a murderer would drive. But suppose Gonson hadn't ratted me out, suppose he actually did know somebody and the man I was meeting was ready and willing to do the job. And suppose he went through with it, and got away clean. Who would they look at?"

"The wife."

"And how well would I hold up? I could probably make it through an hour or so of interrogation, and then I could let it dawn on me that I probably ought to have a lawyer, and after that there wouldn't be any more questions. But if they kept digging—"

"They'd find something. And of course there'd be the chance they'd find their way to the man you hired, because even if he's a pro it's a profession that doesn't have terribly high standards. And he could drink and run his mouth, or he could give his girl-friend reason to drop a dime on him."

"It's funny how that expression is still around. If you could even find a pay phone, what good would a dime do you?"

"The point is, he'd give you up in a hot second."

"I know that. So I was lucky twice, that a real hit man didn't show up at the Winn-Dixie, and that the fake hit man decided he'd rather fuck me than score points with the sheriff."

"It was a little more complicated than that."

"I know that," she said. "It wasn't just my pussy. It was my eyes of blue. But you know what I mean, don't you? I want to do this, Jesus I want to do this, but I don't know how serious we really are."

"I drove to Georgia Sunday."

"Why, to get away from this whole business? You got as far as Atlanta before you changed your mind?"

"I didn't get anywhere near Atlanta. I went to a town called Quitman."

"I never heard of it."

"I went to the high school, and isn't that the perfect venue for a gun show? I spent about an hour there, and I came away with two unregistered guns and a box of shells for each of them."

"Two unregistered guns."

"A pistol and a revolver. The pistol's a Ruger, the revolver's a Taurus."

"With Gemini rising, I'll bet. Well, Jesus Christ, Doak. That's a big step, buying the guns."

"But?"

"I don't know. I don't want to be a downer, but— "

"Go ahead."

"Well, could you actually go through with it? I mean there's a difference between buying a gun and pulling the trigger, isn't there?"

"Absolutely."

"You never actually did it, did you? Kill somebody, I mean."

"Yes."

A pause. "Yes as in yes you did, or yes you know what I mean?"

"I killed a man once," he said.

"How did—"

"With a gun. I shot him and he died."

She thought about this. "You were a policeman."

"Uh-huh."

"It was self-defense," she said. "It was in the line of duty."

"That's how it went in the books," he said, "but that's not how it was. I murdered him."

TWENTY-THREE

He'd never told anyone.

He was working a case, knocking on doors on a mixed block on the Lower East Side, the same tenements housing Wall Street guys and corporate lawyers in four-figure monthly rentals alongside rent-controlled tenants who paid less for rent each month than their yuppie neighbors spent on sushi.

He could remember when you didn't walk on that block if you didn't have to, and now the storefronts were all designer clothes and vegan restaurants.

He was in a building, going door to door, trying to find someone who might have had eyes on the street three nights earlier when somebody gave a young man named Raisin Little a double-tap with a .22. Raisin had a yellow sheet that ran to drug busts, and it was a fair bet that whoever shot him was in the same line of work. As far as Doak was concerned it was a PSH, a public-service homicide, but you did what you could to clear those, too.

And gentrification made that a little more possible than it might have been in the old days, because the new people didn't know that you weren't supposed to talk to the cops.

The woman in 3-G was a junior copywriter at a Madison Avenue agency but was thinking of bailing on that because a couple of friends were starting a web-based company and wanted her to go in with them, and it sounded like fun, and there was always the chance it would work and somebody would buy them out for like a billion dollars. I mean it could happen, right?

And no, she'd heard about the shooting, because how could you not? It had happened right across the street, and she was home and heard the gunfire, or at least she thought now that she must have heard it, but you heard loud noises all the time, and if she even thought about it she thought it was a car back-firing or kids throwing firecrackers, and could someone please tell her what was it anyway with Chinese kids and firecrackers?

So if what she heard was in fact the end of Little Raisin (she got the name turned around, but so did one of the tabloids), well, she never looked out the window to see what was going on, and if she had she probably wouldn't have been able to see anything anyway and—

A woman screamed.

Not on TV, not out on the street. It was right there in that apartment, or maybe next door, and—

"Oh, God," the copywriter said. "They're at it again. The fun couple in 3-F, and I know he's going to kill her one of these days."

Another scream, and the sound of something banging into something. Furniture overturned.

"I keep thinking maybe I should call the police, but I don't know, I have to live next to them, and—was that a gunshot?"

It was, and it was followed by another gunshot, and Doak was out in the hall now, his .38 drawn. He tried the knob, and when the door didn't open he reared back to kick it in.

It must have been just a snap-lock holding it, because the door burst open, and just as it did there was a gunshot and a bullet sailed past him on the left, about shoulder high.

He saw a huge man, barefoot, wild-eyed, wearing stained baggy sweat pants and no shirt, with a gun in his hand.

"Police! Don't move!"

That was what you were trained to shout, and he shouted it

loud and clear, and the guy heard him and didn't have to think it over. He swung toward Doak and pointed the gun at him and squeezed the trigger, all before Doak's brain could tell his hand to point and shoot.

He thought, *I'm dead.*

And heard the hammer click on an empty chamber.

The guy grinned, he fucking *grinned*, and tossed the gun aside. "No bullets," he said, and threw his hands in the air, palms facing forward. "No bullets. Bitch got 'em all."

Nodding to his left, where a woman lay slumped against the wall while her blood pooled on the floor around her. You didn't need to take her pulse to know she was gone.

And that was the moment, frozen in time. The man with his hands in the air, that grin on his face, mocking his captor with his act of surrender.

But a good collar, a great collar. Too late to do the woman any good, but there had never been a chance to do anything for her, and at least he could take in the man who'd killed her. Get him to put his hands on the wall, get him to move his feet away from the wall, grab his hands one at a time, cuff them behind his back.

And call it in.

That grin, that fucking grin on his face—

The .38 bucked in his hand.

"Three times," he said. "I pulled the trigger three times, bam-bam-bam, I put three in his chest, grouped them so close together your hand could have covered all three at once. Did I say he didn't have a shirt on?"

"Yes."

"Hardly any hair on his chest, just maybe a dozen wispy hairs right in the middle. He was such an animal you'd expect him to have a pelt like a bear, but no. His skin was fishbelly white, too, like he never left the house in the daytime."

She sat there, letting him tell it.

He said, "I made a conscious decision. I knew what to do—cuff the fucker, call it in—and instead I went ahead and shot him dead. Bam-bam-bam, and I got him in the heart, and I think he must have been dead before he even knew he'd been shot.

"I looked around, half-expecting to see the copywriter from next door in the hallway. But she'd had the sense to stay where she was, in fact she'd locked herself in. I was all by myself with a dead man and a dead woman. He'd killed her and I killed him and nobody saw a thing.

"He'd tossed the gun halfway across the room. I didn't put it in his hand but I did the next best thing, nudging it with my foot, steering it to where it might have fallen if he'd been holding it when he was shot.

"Then I called it in and waited for the place to fill up with cops.

"I probably would have been all right anyway, but I caught a break. It turned out there were two live cartridges in his gun. It was a six-shot revolver, and I don't know if he spun the cylinder at some point or if he'd only loaded some chambers, but when the gun clicked on a spent cartridge, all he had to do was keep pulling the trigger and he'd have hit a live one.

"If he'd known that he might have killed me. But he didn't and he tossed the gun, and when they examined the weapon there was no way to guess what had actually gone down, because the loaded gun fit the story I was telling. Which is that he was shooting at me, and they dug the one round out of the wall in the hallway, and that he'd have kept on firing at me if I hadn't shot him first."

"So you were all right."

"Any time you discharge your weapon," he said, "there's a lot of shit you go through. They take it away, and you're in for a stretch of desk duty until the formal inquiry's completed. As far as the tabloids were concerned I was a hero cop, at least for a couple of days. And I got through the inquiry without any real trouble. Why hadn't I called for backup? Because I never had a chance. I'd been doing routine canvassing, looking for a witness to the Raisin Little shooting, and my partner was off doing the same thing in a building across the street, because it didn't take two people to knock on a door when there was no reason to expect anything other than a law-abiding citizen on the other side of it. So yeah, I was all right. I'd justifiably used deadly force in self-defense."

"But you don't think it was self-defense."

"I think it's fine they called it that way, and there really wasn't any other way they could have called it. But no, it wasn't self-defense, not once he tossed the gun."

"You were already set to fire, and it was too late to hold yourself back."

He shook his head. "No. I've thought about this enough to be able to say for sure. I had time to think about it, just a second or two but that was plenty of time. And I knew not to pull the trigger, and I went ahead and did it anyway."

"Three times."

"Uh huh. Bam-bam-bam. One of the hoops they made me jump through was a series of sessions with a department psychiatrist. She didn't get the story you're getting, she got the official version. She asked me how I felt about it, and I told her what I figured she wanted to hear. Glad to be alive, sorry I'd had to take a life, sorry I couldn't have been there in time to prevent the woman's death. That last line was true, anyway."

"And not the others?"

"Well, it's true I was glad to be alive. The only problem she had with me is she was concerned by my lack of affect. When I saw the report I read it wrong, I thought she meant I was in-effective, and I didn't see how it applied. But I think she meant my attitude didn't match my words, that I didn't seem to have processed the experience."

"How did you feel?"

"Glad he was dead, glad I'd made him that way. I'd have been just as happy not to go through all the crap that came after it, but it was worth it." He thought for a moment. "How I felt—it didn't have all that much to do with who he was and what he did. Here's what you have to know. I liked it."

"You liked—"

"I liked the feeling. I liked pulling the trigger, I liked watching the man die. It was like coming."

"Honestly?"

"I don't know if I can describe it properly. It was like an orgasm, but it wasn't sexual. It had nothing to do with my dick, nothing to do with sex, really."

"Jesus," she said.

"Yeah, really. So if I lacked affect when I talked to the shrink, maybe that had something to do with it. What I did, I wound up putting in for retirement a little earlier than I'd planned. My marriage coming apart was a factor, plus I got caught up in something unrelated, an Internal Affairs investigation of a former partner of mine that got me a little bit tarred with the same brush. But the shooting, which absolutely went into the books as a righteous use of deadly force, it played a role."

"How?"

"Because once they gave me my gun back," he said, "I figured I'd look for an excuse to use it. Or I'd be afraid I was looking for an excuse, and that would hold me back and keep me from defending myself when I really needed to. If you walk around questioning yourself—"

"Yes, I can see what that would be like."

"So now you know something about me you didn't know an hour ago. Am I really on board for killing your husband? When the time comes, will I be able to pull the trigger? Hell, yes, I'll be up to it. I'll enjoy it."

TWENTY-FOUR

Murder was easy. The tricky part was getting away with it.

He spent the next several days trying to work out a way. The problem, of course, was that her willingness to pay to have her husband murdered was already a matter of record.

The script he'd written, the lines he'd given her, had amended the record so that she'd called off the putative killer and denied that she'd ever been serious about it. And Sheriff Radburn bought the scene he'd staged, or part of it. Yes, she'd called it off, but that hadn't convinced him that she didn't actively desire George Otterbein's death, and wouldn't eventually try to make it happen.

And when it did, she was the first person they'd want to talk to. That was basic, you always looked first to the surviving spouse, and with a far more skeptical eye than the NYPD shrink had turned on Doak's affect, or lack thereof. Did the Widow Otterbein seem unaffected? Did she profess shock, but never shed a single tear? Did the tears flow like an open faucet, but remain somehow unconvincing? Was she too emotional? Was she not emotional enough?

Was she too quick to call for an attorney? Was she not quick enough, as if overly concerned how it might look to lawyer up before the body was cold?

Would she consent to a polygraph test? Her lawyer would shoot that down, but suppose they asked her before he got there? It wasn't evidence, but there were plenty of ways they could hang her with it. They'd make what they wanted out of it, believing the jagged graph when it called her a liar, dismissing it as bad science if it backed her up.

And maybe you couldn't point to it in a courtroom, but you could leak the results when it suited your purpose, so that the jury pool wound up awash with men and women who knew she'd taken a lie detector test, and knew too that she'd failed it.

A call on the Lisa phone:

"Hi."

"Hi."

"Darling, I've got good news and bad news."

"Uh, I suppose you should tell me the bad news first."

"It's the same news."

"I don't—"

"I'm being a pain in the ass, aren't I? I'm sorry. I'm not pregnant."

"Well, that's good news, isn't it? So how is it also bad news?"

"Think about it, Sherlock."

"Oh."

"Right. So let's just postpone our next get-together, because, well, you do get the picture, don't you?"

"You know, even if we don't do anything—"

"Not to mention that there are other things we could do, and they're all things I'm very fond of, believe me. But I'm bitchy and blotchy and I've got cramps and I'm totally not in the mood. So we'll have a little five-day vacation, and in the meantime why don't you call one of your girlfriends?"

"How did girlfriends get to be plural? There's just the one."

"Real Estate Girl, the one with the oh-so-fabulous stories, except that would make them fables, and fables have to have morals. Which her stories don't, and neither does she, and neither do we, either one of us, and isn't that nice? Call her up and get her to tell you a story, and in a few days you can tell it to me. Or you know what? Bring her along and she can entertain us both. You've gone quiet. Don't tell me you're shocked."

"I didn't know you were into that."

"Girls? Not in years, and it was never really what I was about, but women's bodies are nice, aren't they?"

"I've always thought so."

"Well, they just are, and it's not like I'd forget what to do. When you come right down to it, what's the difference between eating pussy and riding a bicycle?"

"Uh—"

"That's a rhetorical question, darling. You don't have to answer it. And if I do forget, I'll just do her the way you do me. You know who I'd really like to do? Roberta, but I forget her last name. You know who I mean. Pregnant Girl."

"You've never even seen her."

"I haven't seen Barbie Doll either. *You've* seen her, but you haven't done anything about it, and I don't know what you're waiting for. How long before she has the kid?"

"I don't know. A couple of months."

"Well, there's time, but still. I'm sure Real Estate Girl's great, but I want Pregnant Girl. You know why?"

"Why?"

"Because I have the feeling we could get Barb to do anything, and she'd be up for it."

"You could be right."

"And Pregnant Girl wouldn't be up for it, but we could make her do it anyway. And maybe she'd like it and maybe she wouldn't, and either way we'd have a good time. *Now* you're shocked. But you still love me, don't you?"

✿

Murder was easy. But how did you get away with it?

No alibi could save her. She could be at a state dinner at the White House when her husband was killed, and they'd haul her in just the same, and be sure she'd had a hand in it. And somewhere along the way they'd take a look at him.

And even if they both held up, and there were no witnesses and zero physical evidence, Radburn and his fellows in law enforcement would know.

He thought about the movie, *Double Indemnity*. Thought about Edward G. Robinson, dogged and resourceful. Radburn was a good old country boy, enjoying his meals and his TV, but would he be any less dogged? Any less resourceful?

No evidence? Nothing that would stand up in court?

The Otterbein children could still file a wrongful death suit. The standards of proof were very different in civil court, and you didn't need the unanimous agreement of the jurors. If you had a preponderance of the evidence and the requisite number of jurors, you got your decision.

And it would keep her from collecting a dime. The insurance company would freeze her claim or deny it outright, and there'd be no inheritance. All she'd wind up with, along with her widow's weeds, was a reputation that would cling to her like a bad smell for the rest of her life.

Lisa Yarrow. Her husband was murdered, you know. Oh, they could never prove anything, but she was behind it. I mean, it was common knowledge.

Moving away wouldn't help. Not with the 24-hour news cycle, not with CNN and MSNBC, not with Nancy Grace and *American Justice* and three or four cable channels with round-the-clock true crime shows. Not with the fucking internet.

"He can run but he can't hide." Joe Louis had said that of Billy Conn, and he'd been talking about a boxing ring twenty feet square. Now it was true of the whole world. You could run, but you couldn't hide.

So how could you get away with it?

He remembered a lecture at John Jay, a retired medical examiner talking about his life's work. "The best way to commit murder and get away with it," he said, "is to make it look like something other than murder. If it goes in the books as natural or accidental death, nobody's going to put you in jail for it.

"So how do you achieve that enviable result? Well, there are two very good ways, and the first is to push the victim from a high window. From a sufficient height, the chances of survival are virtually nil. And, in the absence of witnesses, there's no way anybody can possibly tell whether the late lamented jumped or fell or was pushed."

And the fellow had waited for someone to ask him the other very good way.

"Oh, that's simple," he'd said, when the question came. "Nothing to it, really. Just commit your homicide in Chicago."

That got the expected laugh, and made it clear what opinion the ME held of his counterpart in Cook County. And finding a high enough window within fifty miles of Gallatin County was about as feasible as hauling George Otterbein to Chicago and drowning him in Lake Michigan.

Still, there had to be a way.

He put in time online, doing all manner of searches, then dutifully clearing his history and deleting cookies. With his police background and his present line of work, he had legitimate reasons to bone up on forensics, but even so he didn't want to leave a trail.

His amateur dusting and cleaning would do for now. And

when it was all over, assuming it went as he intended for it to go, he might want to take an extra precaution and drop his laptop—or at the very least the hard drive—into the creek behind the house. The brackish water would finish the job.

Forensics. He'd watched the cop shows, the fictional ones like *CSI* and *Law & Order*, and he knew that they drove real-life cops and prosecutors nuts, because it was all so much easier on TV. Most departments didn't have the resources for that kind of testing, especially in a North Florida backwater.

But there was still DNA, wherever you were. And there were still tox screens. And if George Otterbein died in a car crash, somebody would give the vehicle the automotive equivalent of an all-out autopsy, which is what George would get if he had a heart attack or stroked out or drowned in the bathtub.

Okay, nobody said this was going to be easy.

TWENTY-FIVE

He left the house, drove into town, caught Sheriff Radburn in his office. "Nothing," he reported. "If there's a boyfriend, he must be living in her attic. I leave her alone most of the time, but whenever I track her there's nothing doing. She goes shopping, she gets her hair done, she goes to work, she goes home. I'm wasting my time and the county's money."

"But not too much of either, I don't suppose."

"No, and some of it I won't bill for. I got on her tail the other day and she led me to a mall way the hell south of town. There was a movie house at one end of it, and that's where she went."

"So you turned around and came home?"

"No, I watched the movie, and I'm not planning to bill the county for my ticket."

"Well, that's good to know."

"There's something else you should know," he said. "I dropped in on George Otterbein a few days ago. I wanted a look at him, so I turned up at his office with some story about a missing heir with the same name."

"Oh?"

"He poured me a drink and listened to what I had to say, and it didn't lead anywhere because there was nowhere for it to lead. And then a few days later he called me and hired me."

The sheriff leaned back in his chair. "To check on his wife," he said.

"No, he never even mentioned her. What he wanted was for me to run some background checks on some of his tenants. I like to call it legwork, but the fingers get more exercise than the legs."

"How's that?"

He mimed typing. "They do the walking," he said, "through the internet. The point is, if I'm working for him—"

"You shouldn't be investigating his wife."

"I'm not sure of the ethics of it," he said, "but it's not as though I was getting anywhere."

"No, Doak, and I'm beginning to agree with you that there's nowhere to get. I think she was serious enough when she told Gonson to set her up with a hit man, and I think something scared her off. It's beginning to look like she's staying scared."

"Or just realized murder's a bigger step than she's prepared to take."

"Or that," Radburn said. "Oh, if George turns up with a couple of bullets in him, she's the first person I'll want to talk to. Think it'll happen?"

"No."

"Neither do I. Meantime, at least you got yourself a client."

He drove from Radburn's office to Stapleton Terrace and parked where he could keep an eye on the house. There was a single car parked out in front, a Korean compact that he recognized as Ashley Hannon's.

Go and get yourself pregnant, he thought, and Georgie Boy'll spring for a Lexus.

He checked his watch. Just past ten-thirty, and maybe she was a lady of leisure, maybe she never rolled out of bed before noon. Or maybe she was out jogging. She was young and fit, and people were crazy enough to do that sort of thing, even in Florida with summer coming on.

No, there she was, walking out her front door, dressed like those Eastern European girls who'd bored him senseless playing tennis on TV. The same blonde hair, but hers was curly. A short white skirt, a white top. No headband, and no tennis racquet, either, just a canvas tote bag over her shoulder and a set of keys in her hand, and she triggered the remote to unlock the car door, got in it and drove off.

George had given him a key, but not without getting an explanation first. Two of them, in fact, because the first one Doak floated got shot down.

"No tapes," he said. "You think I want to be on any damn tape recording?"

"It's the best way to be sure she's not seeing anyone," he said, "but I can understand that privacy's a legitimate concern. I'll still need access, though. I assume she has a computer."

Well, of course she did. Who didn't nowadays?

"If she's like most people," he said, "her whole life'll be on it, just waiting to be downloaded. I'll be in and out of there in no time at all, and then you can have your key back."

Right.

He gave her time now to remember what she'd forgotten and come back for it. When this didn't happen, he picked up his clipboard for camouflage and walked to the front door. He rang the bell, because you didn't want to take anything for granted, and when it went unanswered he used the key and let himself in.

What furniture there was looked as if it had been ordered all at once from Walmart or Ikea—everything white, everything new, and none of it built to last. The one thing that wasn't white was her portable massage table, folded and propped against a living-room wall. Her Mac laptop rested on a dinette table in the small kitchen. He booted it up, and the home page supplied her daily horoscope.

He plugged a flash drive into a port and dumped her hard drive onto it.

While the life and times of Ashley Hannon were busy reproducing themselves on the Kingston flash drive that lived on his keychain, Doak climbed the stairs to the bedroom. More white furniture—a six-drawer dresser, a queen-size captain's bed with drawers on both sides.

She hadn't made the bed, and one pillow still held the impression of her head. He picked it up, inhaled her scent. For an instant he had the sense that he was being observed, and then his eyes met those of a teddy bear propped on the other pillow. The bear was dressed in striped overalls and a matching railroader's cap, and looked as though he'd seen it all.

He put the pillow back, then took the microphone from his pocket and looked for a place to mount it. It was not much larger than his flash drive, and the underside of the bed would have been a logical spot for it, but the bed's platform sat flush on the floor.

He opened drawers until he found one that held blankets. Barring a cold snap, there'd be no reason to open the drawer—and there wouldn't be any cold weather for a while, not in a Florida summer.

He set up the mike all the way in the back of the drawer, on top of a blanket; the battery-operated receiver went in the crawl space, which he reached by pushing up a panel in the hall. A quick look showed she had nothing stored up there, and thus no reason to come upon the receiver.

It would work, he thought, but did it have to? If he hadn't already owned the equipment he wouldn't have bothered.

He opened her closet, rummaged through her clothes. Once again he found himself breathing in her scent, and he let himself imagine her body, all firm toned flesh, with a puff of blonde curls at the juncture of her thighs.

He stood there, let himself feel what he was feeling...

And then there was the sound of a car outside, braking to a stop.

His mind raced. If it was her, she'd be in the house before he could let himself out of it. He would have to lurk in one room and wait for a chance to slip past her, but how could he realistically expect to get out without being seen?

And, Jesus, his flash drive was still plugged into her Mac, where she couldn't miss seeing it.

So he didn't have much choice, did he? He'd plant himself behind the bedroom, waiting for her to come upstairs, hoping she'd walk right past the computer, either not noticing it was turned on or thinking she must have left it like that. She'd come into the bedroom and he'd take her from behind.

And what? Hit her in the head, hard enough to knock her out? No, safer and more certain to clap one hand over her mouth and wrap his other arm around her neck, putting her gently to sleep with a choke hold.

He let himself visualize it all, her body struggling in his grasp, then relaxing as she lost consciousness. And pushed the image aside to listen for her key in the lock, for the door opening.

When he didn't hear it he went to the window. The car at the curb was not Ashley Hannon's Hyundai but a Dodge minivan, from which a black woman was lifting a sack of groceries while two of her children made a run for the swing set.

Jesus.

He left the bedroom as he'd found it, went downstairs, retrieved his flash drive and shut down her computer, then let himself out of the house. The neighbor woman was putting away her groceries, he could hear her through the screen door. Her son was pushing his sister on the swing, and they were too involved in what they were doing to pay attention to a middle-aged white man carrying a clipboard.

He got in his car and drove around the corner, stopped in front of a house not all that different from the one he'd just left. He breathed deeply, in and out, and thought how relieved he'd felt at the sight of the minivan.

Relief touched with disappointment.

Because, the fear and tension notwithstanding, he'd wanted her to come up the stairs and into the bedroom, wanted to clap a hand over her little mouth before she knew what was happening, wanted to choke her until she blacked out and went limp in his arms.

"Choke me, will you? Come on, how tricky is that? Use both hands, put 'em around my throat, and choke me a little. Not too hard. Oh, that's nice. A little harder, just a little bit. Oh, yeah."

And then what? Lower her to the floor, slip a hand under that skimpy white skirt, touch her through her panties. Maybe reach inside her panties, give her a little finger wave.

He was hard thinking about it.

Well, he could do something about that. He didn't even have to go home for the clipboard.

TWENTY-SIX

"I'm sorry to bother you, Mrs. Ellison. I thought I had all the information my client required, but it turns out I have some more questions."

No makeup, and this time he noticed that her ears were pierced for earrings, but that she wasn't wearing any. Her housedress was almost identical to the one she'd worn before, and stretched at least as tight over the full breasts and round belly.

"But this can't be a good time for you," he went on. "What time does your boy go for his nap?"

"Oh," she said. "It depends, but usually around noon or a little after. But you don't have to—"

"It's eleven-thirty," he said. "Suppose I come back, oh, forty-five minutes from now? That would be at twelve-fifteen. Would that be all right?"

He didn't wait for an answer, just flashed her a smile and turned to walk to his car. He didn't look back, didn't see her again until he was back behind the wheel of the Monte Carlo. Then he caught sight of her, still standing in the doorway, looking at him.

He was right on time, and when she opened the door to his knock he explained that he hadn't wanted to ring the bell for fear of waking her son.

"Not much chance of that," she said. "Once he's asleep, you could shoot off a cannon next to him and he wouldn't hear it."

In the living room, he took the same seat he'd had on his earlier visit. "Ah, this is nice," he said. "It's warm out there."

"I've been inside all day," she said.

"Well, don't be in a rush to go out. A person can raise a thirst out there."

"Would you care for some iced tea?"

"Oh, you don't have to do go to the trouble."

"It's no trouble. There's a pitcher in the refrigerator."

"Well, if you're having some yourself, Mrs. Ellison."

She came back with two glasses of iced tea. He took a sip and exclaimed over it, and she said it was just from a mix, she hadn't really done anything but stir it up.

He said, "You know what would really pep this up—" and then waved a dismissive hand, cutting off his own remark. She looked at him, puzzled, and he said, "I was just thinking a touch of vodka would make this something special. But that's out of line."

"I think there's some vodka."

"Oh, please, you don't have to—"

"In fact I'm sure there is," she said, and came back to hand him a half-full bottle of Absolut. He uncapped it, then stopped himself from pouring. "Only if you'll join me," he said.

"Oh, I wish," she said, and patted her stomach.

"I didn't even think."

"But please, have some yourself."

"Oh, I don't know," he said. "I hate to drink alone. All these months and you've never had a single sip?"

"Well," she said.

"Oh?"

"Once or twice," she admitted. "I'm not supposed to, but one drink doesn't really hurt, especially in the third trimester."

"Well, in that case—"

"Only a drop," she said, and smiled.

And they talked—about what a hot summer it was likely to be, and what this year's hurricane season might amount to, and how a touch of vodka really brightened up a glass of iced tea, especially when the tea was pre-sweetened.

And then she said, "But you had questions you wanted to ask me."

"Oh, indeed I do. About your neighbor."

"I don't really know that much," she said, "but just go ahead and ask me anything."

"I'm particularly interested in his relationship," he said. "With his wife."

"There's nothing wrong with it," she said. "Not so far as I can tell."

"But what do you know about its more intimate aspects?"

She frowned. "Gee, next to nothing. What do you mean?"

"Well," he said, "there are things I don't suppose you can know, but I get the sense that you're an intuitive person. That's true, isn't it?"

"I suppose so."

"Women tend to be," he said, "and I believe there's scientific evidence that a woman's intuition is enhanced by, well, by your current state." And when she looked puzzled, he clarified what he meant by touching her gently on her stomach, leaving his hand there for only a fraction of a second longer than he had to.

"Oh," she said.

"So what you sense about their relationship might be surprisingly valid."

"Well—"

"So what do you figure the two of them do in bed?"

"Oh, God, I mean I have no idea! I couldn't even guess."

"Oh, sure you could. Do you suppose he eats her pussy?"

She stared at him.

He leaned forward, held her eyes with his, put a hand on her thigh, felt the warmth of her flesh through the thin cotton.

"I wonder if he does," he said, his voice soft but insistent. "I wonder if he enjoys it as much as I'll enjoy eating yours."

"I can't believe what I'm hearing."

"Oh, sure you can."

"I think you'd better go. Now, right now. I want you to go."

"That's not what you want."

"You have no idea what I want!"

"Oh, I have a pretty good idea," he said, and his hand moved up and down on her thigh. "No makeup and no lipstick, and no earrings either, but you're wearing perfume now and you weren't wearing any an hour ago. You tucked him in for his nap and then quick as a bunny you dabbed on a little perfume. Where did you put it, Bobbie? Behind your pretty little ears? Between your big juicy tits?"

"Oh, please don't…"

"Not between your legs, because you've got your own smell down there, don't you? I can smell it from here. You're all wet, aren't you? If you don't want it, why are you all wet?"

She just looked at him.

"You made your decision when you put on perfume," he told her, "and you underlined it when you offered me iced tea. And you let me spike your drink. You're pregnant but you were willing to have a drink because you knew it would make it easier for you to go upstairs with me. I could talk you into another drink, but I don't want to get you drunk, I just want to take you upstairs and fuck you."

He stood up, took her hand, drew her unresisting to her feet.

Afterward he lay on his back, spent. She sat beside him and took his genitals in her hands.

"You'll excuse me for a minute," she said. "I want to go to the garage for the pruning shears."

"The women of America would never forgive you."

"They'd give me a medal. Does the moron next door eat his wife's pussy? I couldn't believe you asked me that."

"Well, I wanted to get your attention."

"You already had it. What on earth made you think you could get me in bed? And don't tell me the perfume, I know all about the perfume. You already decided before you showed up on my doorstep this morning."

"I was playing a hunch."

"What's that, female intuition for guys? Something had to give you the idea."

"Maybe the wish was father to the thought. I felt like hitting on you the first time I saw you."

"But I had Eli there for protection. Which is why you asked about his nap time. You're really a very bad man, Mr. Doak Miller."

"I know."

"The perfume wasn't to get you to fuck me. It was so I could pretend something was going to happen, even though I knew it wasn't. I just wanted to feel attractive, you know?"

"You're beautiful."

"Yeah, right. Big as a house, with no lipstick and no makeup."

"And holes in your ears."

"And unoccupied holes in my ears."

"You're very hot," he said. "You may not believe it, but you are."

"But you didn't just think I was hot, you bastard. You thought I was there for the taking. And then you came upstairs with me and played me like a violin."

"More like a cello."

"Nice. I really ought to cut it off, you know. I could keep it in the icebox as a souvenir and suck on it whenever the mood came over me. Of course I could do that now, couldn't I?"

"Don't expect miracles. I think you got it all the first time."

"Oh, yeah? Is that what you think, mister?"

*

"I guess I can claim to be reasonably good at that," she said. "I ought to be. When I'm like this, that's all he wants."

"He doesn't—"

"Do anything else? No, that's it. From the first time I missed my period with Eli, and then we got a fresh start until I got pregnant with Portia."

"That's a nice name."

"Thank you. I'm in charge of names in this house. The ones he comes up with are either common as dirt or from another planet altogether. But no, all he wants when I'm pregnant is my mouth. He *says* it's because he's phobic on the subject of injuring me or the baby, but I don't think I believe him."

"Maybe he just likes getting his cock sucked."

"I hope that's it, because the other possibility is he finds me unappealing. But you don't."

"You figured that out, did you?"

"Uh-huh. Can I ask you something? Why is it such a big deal to guys if the girl swallows?"

"I don't know."

"Because by the time she does or doesn't swallow, the act's over, right? Once you come in my mouth, what's it matter whether it winds up in my stomach or a Kleenex?"

"I never gave it much thought," he said. "But spitting it out, that's sort of a form of rejection, isn't it?"

"I guess. I mean, if I coughed and spat and made sickening noises and threw up, I can see where that would seem like rejection. I wonder if it has something to do with getting pregnant."

"I don't think you can actually—"

"Duh. But, you know, symbolically. Swallowing equals acceptance of the seed."

"You swallowed," he said. "Were you getting symbolically pregnant?"

"I'm just a greedy little pig who likes her protein. Okay, here's another question. When you were inside me and you had hold of my belly, did you feel her kicking?"

"I did."

"Was that nice?"

"It was interesting."

"I like that you could feel it. And your cum tastes yummy, by the way. Cinnamon."

"Really? I can't think—oh, I had a latte, they sprinkled cinnamon on top."

"I'm gonna have to remember that. I'll have to feed him some cinnamon, and then I can make this remarkable discovery. 'Honey, guess what?' Oh, Jesus, it's time for you to be on your way. Didn't you hear that?"

"What?"

"Just now. There. Eli, talking to his animals. I could hear him because I'm his mommy. And in a minute he'll get louder and they'll be able to hear him next door. Get dressed, and can you find your own way out? Because I'd just as soon as he doesn't see you."

"Sure."

"And this was fun, and nobody got hurt, and I don't have to worry about getting pregnant. But all the same we're not going to do it again. Okay? Can we agree on that?"

TWENTY-SEVEN

Back home he plugged the flash drive into a free port and had a look at what he'd dumped from Ashley Hannon's computer. He worked directly from the flash drive, careful not to move anything onto his own hard drive. He could open all of her files, he could check the emails she'd sent and received, and all without leaving any enduring traces on his own computer.

What he found was mostly what you'd expect to find, given that this was a woman who chose her daily horoscope as a home page. That alone struck him as more than enough to disqualify her from passing her genetic heritage to an Otterbein scion, but he didn't know that George would see it that way. After all, the man was slipping it to the little darling, and that tended to color a fellow's judgment.

One email thread was interesting. He couldn't tell the correspondent's name, as the email address was no help: hodehoho at hotmail.com. A Cab Calloway fan?

Ashley had two eDresses, AHannon437 at Yahoo, which she used for most of her email, and KurlySadge at Hotmail, her address for hodehoho. And the two of them signed their emails only with initials, when they signed them at all. Ashley's were signed with an A, hodehoho's with a C, which probably didn't stand for either Cab or Calloway.

He decided that C was a woman, and very likely a fellow masseuse. Most of the earlier messages were too brief and cryptic to tell him anything, but lately Ashley's at least were longer.

He could guess why. She'd moved, she didn't know anyone

in this part of the state, and she needed a girlfriend to confide in.

But the confidences were sketchy, with code words and abbreviations he couldn't puzzle out. For a while he thought either or both of them might be considering a move to San Diego, because "SD" kept popping up in the thread, but gradually he managed to crack at least that much of their code.

SD wasn't San Diego, or South Dakota, either. It stood for Sugar Daddy.

So Ashley, the Sagittarian with the head of blonde curls (hence KurlySadge), was under no illusions about the nature of her relationship with the Kitchenware King of Gallatin County. He paid her rent and she kept him happy.

Did she have a clue that Otterbein might have bigger plans for her?

If she did, she'd managed to keep it a secret from her computer. Nothing he found suggested she anticipated anything beyond a transient relationship of convenience with her SD. Relieved of the need to work for a living, she could concentrate on mellowing out and getting her head together, whatever exactly those phrases might mean to her. She could work out regularly at the gym in Perry ("tho lame compared to Gold's in St. Pete, and sauna smells awful!!! Little kids pee on the hot rocks!!!") and try to get back to eating right. ("Tough to be only wannabe-vegan for miles around!!!")

It was tiring, sifting through the drivel on the flash drive, and he couldn't stay interested in the game. Why knock himself out tracking the ruminations of an airhead? He knew all he needed to know about her.

He cracked a beer, turned on the TV.

TCM was all about film noir this week. First *The Postman Always Rings Twice*, the 1946 version. He missed the first ten minutes of it, and there was a moment when he got this weird sense of déjà vu, as if he were watching *Double Indemnity* all over again, but with Lana Turner and John Garfield playing the parts of Barbara Stanwyck and Fred MacMurray.

But of course it was a different movie. It had the same basic set-up—two lovers conspiring to kill her husband—and the same writer had written the novel on which it was based.

And, once again, you knew they wouldn't get away with it.

He watched it all the way through to the end, with Garfield on his way to the gas chamber for the murder of Turner, who in fact had died accidentally. If you managed to get away with one thing, the film seemed to be saying, God would get you for something else.

And, just in case he'd missed the message, the cable channel followed with Jack Nicholson and Jessica Lange in, duh, *The Postman Always Rings Twice*. The same title, the same basic story, remade in 1981 and not all that different for the passage of thirty-five years.

Well, it was in color, if that made a difference. And after the two of them get away with murder yet again, Nicholson has an affair with Anjelica Huston. But he patches it up with Lange, until she dies in a car accident. When that happened to Lana Turner in 1946, Garfield went to the gas chamber because they thought he'd staged the accident—though how they could have gotten the man indicted, let alone convicted and sentenced to death, was beyond Doak's comprehension.

Never mind, he thought. In this version, Nicholson didn't have to worry about the law. His true love was gone forever, after they'd managed to work things out, and the film ended with him in tears over her corpse.

You really couldn't win, could you? If you were Fred MacMurray, you paid for the murder you committed. If you were John Garfield, you got away with one murder but paid anyway. And if you were Jack Nicholson, you got away with everything and wound up with a broken heart.

He turned off the set and went to bed.

He woke up early, clawing his way out of a dream. All he knew was it had been a bad one.

It was still dark, and he'd been up late. He couldn't have managed more than a couple of hours of sleep, and felt as though they'd been mostly surface sleep; when he finally did fall deeply asleep, his reward was a nightmare.

And now he was jarringly awake while the rest of the world slept on around him.

He went out and sat on his dock and waited for the sun to come up. The last thing he'd been thinking about, lying in bed and waiting to drift off, was the latest remake of *Postman*, the one that starred Doak Miller and Lisa Yarrow, the one with George Otterbein cast as the deservedly doomed husband. He knew how to do it, had the solution right there in his mind, but the puzzle pieces wouldn't quite fit into place. He'd fallen asleep turning them this way and that, trying to make it all work.

And evidently his mind had continued the process while he slept, because now he could see it. How they would make it happen, and get away with it.

TWENTY-EIGHT

He called Lisa. His call went straight to voicemail, and he said "Call me" and rang off.

He was working away on the computer when the phone rang. "The little automatic," he said. "With the green grips."

"Malachite."

"Whatever. Is it still in the nightstand?"

"It was the last time I looked. Why?"

"I need it."

"Jesus, are you planning on starting a war? How many guns do you need?"

"Just that one."

"I'm kind of tied up today," she said. "When do you need it?"

"As soon as possible, and you don't have to drive clear to Chiefland to give it to me. You'll be working at the restaurant tonight? Bring it with you, park in your usual spot. Tuck the gun on the floor under the driver's seat, and leave the car unlocked. Can you remember that?"

"I'll write it on the palm of my hand," she said, "just in case it slips my mind. Yes, of course I can remember. But what if it's not in the drawer? I'm not home now, I can't go check."

"Call me when you know one way or the other."

"All right."

"And just leave a message. 'It's there' or 'It's not there.'"

"One if by land and two if by sea."

"If it's there," he said, "take it with you when you leave the house."

"And park in my regular space, and put the gun under the seat."

"And don't lock the car."

"You know, that'll be the hardest part, because locking it is so automatic. But don't worry, I'll remember."

He hadn't told her about Roberta Ellison.

He thought about the omission, and thought about the incident at the Ellison home, while little Eli had his nap. Thought about it and shook his head, pushing the memory aside.

Time to tell her later. She'd call to tell him about the pistol, whether or not she'd found it in the drawer, and that would be time enough to tell her.

He was at the computer when the phone rang, the Lisa phone. He picked it up and held it in his hand and it rang again, and rang a third time.

And went to voicemail.

Where he picked up the message a few minutes later: "It was there, and now it's in my purse."

He played it through again, then erased it.

He timed his drive to the Cattle Baron so that it was just past sunset when he pulled into the lot. He parked, and waited in his car while a party of four made their way to the restaurant entrance. Two men walking together, talking, with the two women a pace or so behind them. Two husbands and their wives, ready to sit down and eat beef.

The Lexus was where he'd expected to find it, and she'd remembered not to lock the door. He reached beneath the left front seat and his hand found the little gun right away. It was a pretty thing, a Baby Browning, and the swirly green grips made it the perfect lady's weapon.

But he could admire it later.

He returned to his Monte Carlo and drove out of the restaurant lot, then found his way to Stapleton Terrace.

❋

There were two cars at the curb, Ashley's Hyundai and the neighbor's minivan. And, in the driveway, a Lincoln Town Car with vanity plates that read GOGO.

He'd seen the car before, parked in a reserved space in front of a three-story red-brick building on Court House Square. George's car, tagged with George's doubled initials.

The lights were on in the bedroom window upstairs. He sat in the Chevy, looked at the car, the house, the upstairs window. He took the little gun out of his pocket and held it in both hands, rubbing the ball of one thumb against the cool green stone.

He put the gun away, drove home.

At the computer, he typed:

OMG, the SD gave me a gun!!! Pretty, too, w/ green stone on the handle. Said it's mallokite (sp?). In case the prowler comes back, but would I even dare to use it? I don't think so!!! If I had two of them they could be earrings but maybe too heavy???

He read it over, highlighted the last sentence and hit Delete. In its place he typed:

All it needs is a pin and I cd wear it as a brooch. Thought about it, changed brooch to broach, changed it back to brooch, and deleted the sentence altogether.

Rewrote the whole thing:

OMG, gift from SD—a gun!!! Pretty swirly green handle. Mallokite (sp?) So I won't worry about prowler, but would I dare use it? I don't think so!!!

Two spaces down he wrote:

Miss you!

And on the next line:

~A~

❋

He got up, used the bathroom, returned to the computer and read it through again. You could overthink this shit, he thought, and what was the point?

Print it out?

No, might as well do it right. He'd done everything right thus far, and this was no time to stop.

He got a sheet from a legal pad, fastened it to his clipboard. Took a ballpoint pen, and was it the same one he'd used to print out his and Lisa's lines? It might be, one Bic was rather like another. Whether it was the same pen or another like it, it would do.

He copied the email draft. Once again he used block caps, but was less concerned about making it readable. He was the only one who'd have to read it.

TWENTY-NINE

He took the Browning out onto the deck, along with the pint of Georgi.

He'd bought the bottle on the way home from the Ellison house, the purchase triggered by the slug of Absolut he'd added to his iced tea. They had all sorts of vodka, Ketel One and Stoli and Grey Goose on the same shelf with the Absolut, but he'd always taken it as a given that vodka was vodka, and any premium you paid was for the label. He'd gone with Georgi, and put it away unopened.

He twisted the cap off now, and took a pull straight from the bottle. He made a face at the taste, but he'd have done the same whatever vodka he was drinking. It tasted, he decided, about the way it was supposed to.

He had another pull, and this time the taste didn't bother him. He capped the bottle, set it down on the deck, and picked up the Browning. He was familiar with the model, had taken one away from a man who'd planned on using it to kill himself. "You saved my life," the poor bastard told him, but he'd done no such thing. The guy had saved his own life when he'd decided not to pull the trigger.

That particular Baby Browning had sported checkered metal grips, and the same thumb-slide safety as the one he was holding now.

He sniffed the muzzle and smelled nothing but a faint trace of gun oil, suggesting it hadn't been fired since its last cleaning. For all he knew it had never been fired, and the last cleaning had taken place when it left the factory.

He removed the six-shot clip, which now held five .25-caliber cartridges. Had Otterbein chambered a round? If so, there was a live cartridge under the hammer, and a trigger pull would discharge it even with the clip removed from the gun.

He'd heard of no end of cases in which someone had been killed with a presumably unloaded weapon, but his instructor at the academy had spoken of two incidents, both in Brooklyn, in which the fatal bullets had been fired by automatic pistols from which the magazines had been removed.

"How can you shoot yourself with an unloaded gun? Answer, it's still loaded. You can take that clip out and throw it in the Gowanus Canal, but if there's a round in the chamber, it's loaded and deadly, and there's a man who shot himself and another who shot his wife, and they both thought for sure they were just clowning around."

Lisa had pressed the Browning's muzzle against her husband's forehead, had described the little O it left impressed into his skin. He looked at the muzzle of the gun, pressed it forcefully against the palm of his left hand, withdrew it and examined the mark it left.

Tried the same thing on his forehead. Right between the eyes, he thought. Right where the little girl in the nursery rhyme had a little curl, right in the middle of her forehead.

His finger on the trigger…

He replaced the clip, put the gun in his lap. He uncapped the pint of Georgi, took another pull, a long one this time. The vodka, he realized for the first time, had the same name as the man he was going to murder. Well, almost. The vodka ended in an I, the man in an E. Georgi was George in Russian, and he wasn't a hundred percent sure of the pronunciation. He'd heard people say Georgie, same as the basic nickname for George, but he'd also heard something along the lines of gay-OR-ghee, with both G's hard. Which was probably how they said it in Russia, but this cheap crap was distilled in the States by your basic American capitalists, so giving it a fancy Russian pronunciation seemed a little precious, didn't it?

He'd just pointed at the bottle. "Yeah," he'd agreed, when the clerk took it off the shelf. "That one."

He took another pull, capped the bottle.

And thought about Pregnant Girl.

She'd led him upstairs, and on the way he ran a hand under her skirt and touched her, and in the bedroom she arranged herself with a pillow under her bottom and her legs wide apart.

He teased her, bringing her right to the edge, then easing off, and she liked the game and went with it, saying *Oh, please, please,* and when he finally let her come she bunched up the bedsheet and jammed it in her mouth to muffle her cries.

He rolled her onto her side and took her from the rear, feeling her bottom against his stomach, putting his right arm around her, his hand on her belly, his left hand on her shoulder. He was rock-hard and ready to burst, but at the same time there was no great urgency, and instead of thrusting he held himself in check and savored the feeling of her moist warmth around him.

And she began a rolling motion of her own, getting into it, going for it herself. *Greedy little pig,* he thought, letting her work, and his eyes centered on the back of her neck.

He moved a hand from her shoulder, let it settle on her neck.

His other hand shifted from her belly, that great round mound of belly, and joined the first hand at her throat.

He thought of Ashley's bedroom, of waiting behind the door for her. And that voice from long ago:

"Choke me, will you? Come on, how tricky is that? Use both hands, put 'em around my throat, and choke me a little. Not too hard. Oh, that's nice. A little harder, just a little bit. Oh, yeah."

He could choke her a little. Phyllis had liked it enough to ask for it, and she couldn't be the only woman in the world who liked it. He could choke Roberta a little, just a little—

No.

No, he didn't want to choke her a little, he wanted to choke her a lot. Once he started, he wouldn't stop.

So he didn't let himself begin.

Instead he made himself take each hand from her throat, and he got his arms around her and his hands on her belly, and he held onto her that way, and matched her movements with his own. His hands could feel it when the baby kicked, but in his mind he still had both hands on her throat, choking the life out of her.

And now he remembered the man he'd killed in the third-floor flat on Suffolk Street, remembered how he'd had only a moment to make his decision, but that moment had been all the time in the world. Time to know he didn't have to pull the trigger, that the man had surrendered, that it was time to cuff him and call it in.

Time to know all that, and time to say the hell with it.

Time to say it not once but three times, bam-bam-bam.

And the feeling it gave him.

We can tell each other everything, Lisa had said. And he'd even been able to tell her about the man he'd shot, about everything connected to it, including the asexual whole-self orgasm it had provided. And she in turn had told him things she'd never told anyone else.

But how could he tell her this?

*

He went to take a last swallow of the vodka, but the bottle was empty. The last pull had evidently finished it, and how come he hadn't noticed as much?

Well, he thought reasonably, the vodka must have had something to do with that. Drink enough of it and it kept you from noticing that it was all gone.

He capped it, but a capped bottle wouldn't sink. It would float at the surface, and that would be fine if there was a message in it, but he didn't have any messages for anybody, not even for himself.

He took the cap off, heaved the bottle, heard the splash. And could only assume it filled with water and sank, because he couldn't see anything out there.

Flipped the cap in after it.

Groped around for the gun. Where the hell was it? Oh, there it was.

Thought about the man on Suffolk Street, thought about Bobbie Jondahl Ellison.

Very different.

Because he'd never regretted the three bullets, bam-bam-bam, grouped so precisely in the center of that bare and nearly hairless chest. The world, he'd thought then and still thought now, was none the worse for no longer having that man in it.

But if his hands had done what they had wanted to do, what they very nearly insisted upon doing, the regret would have been immediate and overpowering. He liked the woman, and had only good feelings for her. A tightass moralist might have been inclined to brand her with a scarlet A for adultery, but only the fucking Taliban would regard that as an offense punishable by death.

His hands hadn't cared. They'd longed to wring her neck.

✿

Now his hands held the little automatic.

Removed the clip.

Pressed the muzzle to his forehead, where it was very likely making a little O that he couldn't see, not without a mirror. Awkward, too, holding the gun in that position. Give yourself a sore shoulder if you weren't careful.

Put it in his mouth, angled up and back. Didn't care for that, either. Took it out of his mouth, held it to his temple.

Now that felt better. Comfortable, and a whole lot more natural.

So?

Time for a little game of Brooklyn Roulette?

He thought about it. A bunch of voices in his head fought for his attention, and one spoke a little more clearly than the others.

He took the gun from his temple, pointed it out across the water, angled it upward a little.

Bam!

The gunshot didn't get him sober. That would have been more than you could reasonably ask of any sound, however dramatic. But it did get his attention, and lift him out of that particular drunken reverie.

He was still holding the gun, and he lowered his eyes and stared at it. The barrel was warm, he noted, but the malachite grips remained cool to the touch.

He'd sniffed it before and smelled nothing but steel and gun oil. Now the air was thick with the reek of spent gunpowder, and he waved a hand in front of his face as if to push the smell aside.

It seemed to him as though the sound of the gunshot was still there to be heard, still echoing audibly off the water. But he was just hearing the shot in his memory. The night air was still, silent.

He waited for a response. Lights going on, car engines, a siren.

Nothing.

Well, it was a fact that his house was set off by itself. He had neighbors, but nobody all that close. And a single gunshot wasn't all that rare in the still of a Florida evening, and this little gun didn't make that loud a noise, for all that it had sounded to him like a cannon going off. From any kind of distance, it could have been a firecracker, could have been a car backfiring, could have been a door slamming. Could have been a gunshot on TV, where God knows there were a lot of them.

He weighed the clip in his hand. It still held five cartridges. He didn't expect to need more than that.

THIRTY

He woke up with a headache and a dry mouth, hauled himself out of bed, swallowed a couple of aspirin and drank a lot of water. By the time he got out of the shower, his headache had subsided and he felt almost human.

He remembered everything.

All of it, clear as a bell, clear as a gunshot echoing off the water. Clearer, really, than it had been to him while it was going on.

Jesus, he'd come awfully close, hadn't he? The gun to his temple, his finger on the trigger. He hadn't known there was a bullet in the chamber, but he'd have found out, wouldn't he? The tiniest bit more pressure on the trigger and—

And it would all have been somebody else's problem, he thought, because he'd be out of it. Assuming the bullet did the job, and didn't just leave him in a profound vegetative state, which everybody agreed was a fate worse than death.

But was it? If you didn't know what was going on, what difference did it make?

Not the right kind of thoughts for a man to be having, not when he had a busy day ahead of him.

When he pulled up within sight of the Stapleton Terrace duplex, both the Hyundai and the minivan stood at the curb. The Lincoln, as he'd expected, was no longer parked in the driveway.

He sat in his car for the better part of an hour. Didn't she have a yoga class this morning? Hadn't she mentioned as much somewhere, maybe in an email to C, aka hodehoho?

Maybe the class was within walking distance and she was there now. Or maybe the class was some other day, and she was already midway through the hour of jogging that was on this morning's agenda.

He could go ring the bell. If she answered, he was a man with a clipboard, looking for Mr. Rupert. Nobody here by that name, she'd say, and he'd say the fellow must have moved out.

He was weighing the pros and cons when the door opened and Ashley emerged, gym bag in hand. She walked briskly to her car, unlocked it with the remote, and drove away.

He gave her five minutes, then let himself into her house.

The first thing he noticed was the fifth of Glenmorangie on the sideboard, the same brand Otterbein kept in his office. It hadn't been there on his last visit.

No need to stop at the liquor store, not with a bottle already on hand. The seal was broken, and a couple of ounces were gone. One good drink, he thought, or two small ones.

No need to boot up her computer, either. She'd left it on. The screen had gone dark, but it brightened as soon as he touched the mouse.

He checked History, saw that her last activity was in her Hotmail account. He went to it, and read that morning's email to hodehoho. Some quality time with SD, she'd reported, and then went on to wonder whether aerobics and yoga might tend to cancel each other out.

He copied from his clipboard, amending the text slightly:

OMG, here's what I forgot to tell you!!! SD had some drinks last nite and then surprised me with an amazing gift—a gun!!! Pretty swirly green handle. Mallokite (sp?) So I won't worry about prowler, but would I dare use it? I don't think so!!!

~A~

He read it over, hit Send.

✦

Upstairs, he retrieved the voice-activated mike from the platform bed's blanket drawer, the receiver from the ceiling crawl
space. Leaving them would establish the notion that Otterbein
had been suspicious of his mistress, but he couldn't do that
without knowing what the mike might have picked up, and he
couldn't spare the time to play it back now.

He returned to the first floor, frowned at the computer on
the dinette table. The only way she'd see the email he'd just
sent on her behalf was if she clicked out of her Inbox and into
her Sent Mail file, and why should she do that?

Of course there was another way she could see it, and that
was if hodehoho read the new message and replied to it. *He
gave you a gun? Whoa. Sounds pretty but pls don't get carried
away and shoot yourself!!!*

Well, he would just have to hope hodehoho didn't check her
email all that compulsively, and took her time replying.

He let himself out, pulled the door shut behind him. On the
way to his car he had the sense that he was being watched, but
avoided turning around until he reached his car. Then he looked
back at the house, just in time to see a curtain drop back in place
in the other half of the duplex.

Ashley's neighbor, taking an interest.

He'd have been just as happy not to have a witness to his
departure. But the woman didn't know him, and had only seen
him from the back. And from where she was, she couldn't have
gotten a good look at his car. Or spotted his license number,
even if she'd been inclined to write it down.

So what might she conclude? Probably that her bouncy blonde
neighbor had more than one boyfriend, and what harm could
that do?

✦

Halfway home, he pulled over and took out his cell phone. The regular one, not the Lisa phone.

He called Otterbein's office, gave his name to the woman who answered. When Otterbein came on the line, he gave the report he figured the man wanted to hear, said he couldn't find anything unsettling to report.

"Her background appears to be everything you could hope for," he said. "No one related to her has committed a felony or misdemeanor in the state of Florida. There's no evidence of mental illness in her family, or any sign of hereditary diseases in her family tree."

Otterbein said that was good.

"And I didn't like to snoop," he went on, "but I had a good look at her computer and her recent emails, and my impression is that she's very pleased with her present situation. In fact I think—"

"Yes?"

"Well, that she cares for you."

And that pleased the man, too.

"I want to have one more look at her hard drive," he said, "but I want to pick the right time. You won't be over there this evening, will you? You will? Good thing I asked, I wouldn't want to show up at the wrong moment. I'll wait until tomorrow or the next day."

Back home, he set up the recorder and played the tape. There were two sequences, and the first and more interesting of the two consisted of an extended monologue of Ashley's. She was doing all the talking, but seemed to be addressing her remarks to someone else, someone who never appeared to respond. She talked about her day, recalled an incident or two from childhood, and went on for quite a while before the penny dropped.

She was talking to her teddy bear.

That brought him up short, the sweet innocence of it. He

stopped the tape and had to sit down. Maybe, he thought, this would be a good time to pull the plug on the whole business. Toss the mike and the recorder where he'd tossed the empty vodka bottle, toss the Baby Browning in after it. Toss the Taurus and the Ruger and the two boxes of shells.

Toss everything, for Christ's sake. The flash drive, with all Ashley's files copied onto it. Toss his own computer while he was at it, and his phones, both of them.

And then just get in the car. Get over to I-75 and just drive north for a couple of hundred miles, and then figure out where to go next. Sheriff Radburn would wonder where he'd gone to, but he wouldn't burst a blood vessel over it. A couple of women would miss him, but not that badly and not for all that long.

As for where he'd wind up, well, it wouldn't be Florida and it wouldn't be New York. But that still left a whole lot of country.

He played the rest of the recording. After she was done talking to the teddy bear, he got to hear her with Otterbein, and they'd evidently got most of their talking out of the way before coming upstairs. Much of what he was able to hear consisted of the two of them shifting position on the bed, and then there was a sequence where Otterbein said, "Oh, that's good, that's good," and Ashley said nothing at all, for reasons that weren't all that difficult to imagine.

Then some more conversation, fading in volume as they dressed and left the bedroom. And then a break, and then a sigh from Ashley, and the words, "Oh, pul-*leeze*, give me a fucking *break*," addressed probably to God, but possibly to the teddy bear.

And then he heard her gargle. And spit.

Well, maybe he wouldn't throw the gun in the creek, or drive the car halfway to Montana. Not just yet, anyway.

THIRTY-ONE

He was stretched out on the couch, not asleep and not awake, while Turner Classic Movies went on plumbing the emotional depths with *In A Lonely Place*. From the first close-up of Bogie's face, you just knew this could only end in tears.

The phone rang.

He picked it up, saw who it was. It rang again while he tried to decide whether or not to let it go to voicemail, and midway through the third ring he picked up.

"I was all set to leave a message," Barb Hamill said.

"Well, if you'd rather—"

"Silly. I was thinking I could come over, actually."

"Hang on," he said, and muted the TV, leaving Bogart and Gloria Grahame in a wordless pantomime.

"You know," she said. "If you feel like company."

"Hell."

"Shall I take that for a no?"

"I've got a client coming," he said. "In about half an hour."

"A client? I hope she's cute."

"It's a man," he said, "and he's a long way from cute. He thinks his wife's cheating on him."

"Is she?"

"If she's not," he said, "it's not for lack of provocation. He's a moron, and his commitment to personal hygiene is sort of tentative."

"Ewww."

"So if you had any ideas of dropping by for threesies—"

"I didn't," she said, "but if I did, you just nipped them in the bud."

"But he won't be here for half an hour," he said. "Are you in your office?"

"In my car, actually."

"Parked?"

"No, driving around."

"And talking on the phone while you're driving? I think this is one of those states where that's against the law."

"It is, but my phone's hands-free. It's still against the law, but how can they tell? I'm not holding a phone, I'm just talking to myself, so the worst they can do is assume I'm crazy."

"Now why would anybody get that idea?"

"I know, it's preposterous, isn't it?"

"Utterly," he said. "Now if you were to park the car—"

"We could have a conversation. Is that what you were going to say?"

"It is, and—"

"And I'll probably want to have my hands free. Did I take the words right out of your mouth?"

"You did."

"Hang on a minute. I think I might like to find a spot where there's a chance I'll have some privacy… Okay, this is good. Are you still there?"

"I'm right here."

"And I'm wearing panties, but…there, now I'm not. Now what are we gonna talk about? I haven't done anything since I saw you, except fake an orgasm with the man himself, and I can't see triggering a real orgasm by telling you about a fake one."

"I've got something to tell you," he said.

"You do? Oh, how nice. Has little Doak been a naughty boy? And was he playing with anybody I know?"

"This was years ago."

"Oh?"

"Back in New York, when I was a cop."

"Tell mama."

"There was his woman I met at a party," he said, and described Phyllis, letting her be a little more attractive than he remembered her. He dropped her cop husband out of the picture, made her a little younger, and had her living at home with her parents.

"She liked to be choked," he said.

"Really?"

"You never heard of that? Yeah, she liked it. When she was getting close, you know."

"To coming."

"Uh-huh. 'Oh, baby, choke me a little. Just a little, not too hard, but choke me.'"

"And you didn't feel weird doing that?"

"No, I sort of liked it. And she would come really hard that way."

"I don't know if I'd like it."

"Well, try to imagine it," he said, "Are you touching yourself?"

"Of course."

"Are you wet?"

"Uh-huh."

"Well, imagine my hands on your neck, just applying the least little bit of pressure. And you're a little bit afraid, because suppose I lose control? But you're also excited, because it's out of your hands now, and all you can do is let go."

"Oh, wow," she said. "I guess I get it. It's a little freaky, though. You'd be inside her and choking her at the same time, huh?"

"You bet."

"Are you hard now, baby? I'll bet you are."

He wasn't. He felt nothing, really, which was interesting in and of itself.

"Like a tree trunk," he said. "Like a rock."

She was breathing hard, moving toward the edge. He waited, and she said, "Then what happened?"

"She got pregnant. Swore it was mine, but how did I know?"

"She was seeing other men?"

"She said no, but I had my suspicions."

Waiting for her to ask.

"What did you do?"

"Well, I went to bed with her. We had to be quiet, you know, because she was still living in her parents' house, and of course I didn't have a place to take her."

"You were married."

"Uh-huh. And she was really nice, you know, with her tits getting bigger because of the pregnancy, and her belly just beginning to swell. You couldn't see it when she was dressed, but it showed when she was naked."

"And you went to bed with her."

"I did," he said, and spun it out for her, describing a round of imaginary foreplay, letting Barb get into it. She'd lost her edge some with the news of the pregnancy, but now she was getting it back.

"And then I was inside her."

"In her pussy."

"No, in her ass," he said, "the way you like it."

"And she liked it, too."

"No," he said, "she never liked it in the ass. In fact she hated it."

"Then why did you—"

"Because *I* liked it," he said. "And what did I care what she liked or didn't like?"

"But—"

"And I got my hands on her throat," he said, "and I choked

her the way she liked to be choked, the little cunt. And all of a sudden she didn't mind that I was fucking her in the ass, she was into it, and she was moving in that nice rocking motion, like you're moving now, aren't you—"

"Oh—"

"And what I do, I just keep squeezing. Both hands, as tight as I can make them, and she starts twitching like a fish on a line, twitching like crazy, and I can feel the cartilage giving way, and I don't stop, I can't stop, and I come in a flood as the life drains right out of her."

A long, long silence.

Then she said, "That was terrible."

"Just a story, babe."

"What on earth made you say all that?"

"Oh, just a change of pace. I thought you'd enjoy it."

"How could you even think that? You just ruined everything. You realize that, don't you?"

"How is anything ruined? Hey, don't tell me you don't know the difference between fantasy and reality. I made up a story, I tried to make it exciting for you."

"It was much too real."

"Well, maybe I'm a better storyteller than I realized."

More silence, and he let it build. Then she said, "I think maybe this whole thing is taking a turn I don't like."

"Oh?"

"Maybe we need a break. Maybe I won't call you for a little while."

Like forever, he thought. He said, "I've got a better idea, Barb. Let me see if I can't get rid of my client, and you can come over. We'll go to bed, and then I'll choke you a little bit—"

"Please stop."

"—and you'll be able to see if you like it, and—"

"I'm hanging up."

"Now why would you want to go and do a thing like that?"

But it was he who pushed the button and ended the conversation. And the relationship with it, he thought, and not a moment too soon.

About time he let go of Barb. His life was complicated enough without her in it.

In a Lonely Place, the sound restored, reached its dark ending. He turned off the set and sat in front of it, his eyes on the blank screen.

After a while he called Lisa, caught her just as she was leaving for work.

"Stay on the floor for your whole shift," he told her. "Be around people. Don't duck out even for a minute, don't make any phone calls."

"On this phone, you mean."

"On any phone. And we're done with these phones. We can't use them anymore, and owning them is dangerous. Do you have any saved messages?"

"Just one. In case I needed to hear your voice."

And what would happen when someone else heard it? He said, "Well, the first thing you do is delete the message."

And he told her the rest—how to dismantle the phone, how to get rid of it. He'd be doing the same with his, he said.

But how would they be able to talk?

"We won't," he said. "Not for a while."

After their last visit to the love nest, he'd watched the Lexus drive off, then spent a few minutes buying some things for cash at J. C. Penney's. Black wash pants, a black hoodie, a pair of black sneakers.

He was wearing his purchases when he left the house. The

Baby Browning with its green stone grips was in one pocket. The Taurus revolver, all its chambers loaded, was in another. His own lawfully registered Smith stayed behind on the closet shelf, while the Ruger nine remained out of easy reach in the kitchen cupboard.

Got in his car, sat behind the wheel with the key unturned in the ignition, going over it all in his mind. Knew it was time, knew what he would do and how he would do it. It wasn't a terribly complicated plan, but the best ones never were.

He had it figured out. He could do it.

He started the car, drove off, turned left at the end of Osprey Drive.

He had a full tank of gas. He had a few hundred dollars in his wallet, a couple of credit cards that were nowhere near maxed out. He could cut east and pick up I-75 and just drive. Be safe to use the credit cards, because nobody would have any reason to be looking for him. Because he hadn't done anything, and he didn't have to do anything, did he?

He'd already ditched the Lisa phone. Wished he'd saved a message, wished he could have heard her voice one more time, but he hadn't, and now he couldn't because the phone was dismantled and discarded.

Just get on the Interstate and go. Forget everything else, blue eyes included, before it was too late.

But it was already too late, wasn't it? Really, truly, wasn't that the final message of all the films he'd been watching? Hadn't it been too late from the beginning?

THIRTY-TWO

On Stapleton Terrace, the neighbors' minivan was parked at the curb. No little Hyundai stood next to it, no Lincoln Town Car hogged the driveway.

He kept going, turned left at the corner, turned left again.

He'd circled the block on an earlier visit. The houses here on this street were all single-family units, with several sporting For Sale signs. One had looked unoccupied, and he was not surprised to find it dark this evening, with no car in its driveway or at the curb.

He parked in front of it, took his keys but left the car unlocked. He skirted the house, walked through back yards and gardens in his dark pants and hoodie, moving lightly in his sneakers, staying in the shadows as much as he could. Here and there a yard had been fenced to confine a child, but he didn't have trouble threading his way through the yards to the rear of the duplex.

He walked around the side, noted the continuing absence of the Hyundai and the Lincoln, then returned to try his key on Ashley Hannon's back door. It fit and turned in the lock, but the door, secured by a separate bolt, wouldn't budge.

Always something, he thought. And it was his own fault. He'd been in the kitchen before, he'd seen the door, and why hadn't he seen the bolt and done something about it?

Why? Because he hadn't thought to look for it. You couldn't think of everything, could you?

You couldn't just stand there, either, or you'd miss your chance to be the first one inside.

He looked through the neighbors' kitchen window, saw through the kitchen to a room where a flat-panel TV was entertaining the whole family.

Good.

He walked around to the front of the house, careful not to make any noise. The screen door stuck, and for a moment he thought it was latched, but how had she managed to leave the house with a door latched in front and another bolted in the back? She was lithe, she was athletic, she could no doubt climb out a window, but why on earth—

No, he discovered, the screen door wasn't latched. It was just stuck, and a slightly firmer pull drew it open.

His key turned the lock without a sound. He slipped inside, drew the door shut.

And stood still, waiting, listening.

Nothing.

He couldn't hear the neighbors moving around. He knew they had the TV on but couldn't swear it wasn't muted, as no sound reached him through the wall. A side-by-side duplex had a great advantage over a more conventional two-family house; you could figure on a barrier of concrete block between the two apartments, enough to insulate each tenant from the sound created by the other.

Not much chance anyone could hear him, not with the windows closed and the air conditioning on.

An hour and a half later he drew the bolt that had kept him from opening the kitchen door. He retraced his steps through the back yards, and he had almost reached his entry point when a dog started barking.

He dropped to the ground, rolled into a patch of deeper shade. The dog kept it up, and a light went on above the back door two houses over. The door opened, and a man stepped out onto his brightly lit back stoop and shined a flashlight this way and that.

Then the flashlight went out, and the man went back inside and turned off the exterior light. Doak could hear him cursing the dog for barking at nothing.

He went to his car, took a couple of minutes to catch his breath, and headed home.

He sat up late, waiting for the phone to ring, waiting for a knock on the door.

Nothing.

He went to bed, couldn't sleep, got up and put the TV on. Watched without watching. Cracked a beer, drank half of it poured the rest down the sink.

Went to bed again, a few hours before dawn, and this time he slept.

THIRTY-THREE

The phone. Radburn, and for a change the Sheriff had placed the call himself. "You met the man," he said without preamble. "Saw him more recently than I did. You see this coming?"

He held on to the phone, drew a breath.

"Doak? You there?"

"I'm here," he said, "but I don't know what you're talking about. What man, and see what coming?"

"You just woke up."

"When the phone rang."

"So you haven't heard," Radburn said.

The neighbor had phoned it in, the husband, up in the middle of the night, letting his wife sleep while he soothed a child with a bad dream.

Sitting in the living room, holding the little girl on his lap, trying to think of a story to tell her, he'd looked out the window and seen the big Lincoln in the driveway.

He'd see the car from time to time, but never much past midnight, and here it was getting on for dawn.

Still, nothing alarming about a car in a driveway, where it had every right to be. But when he'd put his daughter back to bed he was wide awake and felt like a cigarette, and his wife didn't like him smoking in the house.

So he stepped outside, and saw all the lights on next door, and that was at least as unusual as the car in the driveway. He went over to the front door, and noted that the TV was on, and playing loud. He hadn't been able to hear it inside his house, but he could hear it now.

Now you mind your own business, he told himself. But maybe somebody was hurt, maybe the old man's heart went on him, and maybe this *was* his business, maybe there was some help he could offer. He knocked on the door, and when his knock went unanswered he rang the bell. Then he rang it a second time, and turned away when no one responded, but something made him try the knob, and the door opened to his touch.

He called out a few times, asking if anybody was home, asking if everything was all right. And then the smell reached him, and he knew that they were home, and that everything was definitely not all right.

"Her clothes were ripped," Radburn said, "and she had bruises on her face and body, but her face was so distorted from strangulation that it was hard to tell how much of a beating she took.

"Ashley Hannon, that's her name. His tenant, that's how he had her listed, but there's no record of her ever writing out a rent check. I'd say she paid her rent via the barter system, and he was there collecting it when something went wrong.

"He had a bottle there and he'd been drinking, and maybe one of 'em said something the other one didn't like, but one way or another I guess they got into it.

"Hard to put things in sequence, but we know that he punched her and slapped her, and she picked up a gun and shot him. Thing is, it looked like a girl's gun, this cute little toy with malachite grips, which I've seen on fancy knives but never before on a handgun. Pearl, yes—which is to say mother of pearl, and ivory, from back when you could import it, but never malachite. It's a .25-caliber automatic, sized to fit in a vest pocket, and when we checked the registration it turns out he bought it himself almost four years ago.

"And when we look a little further, we find out George gave her the gun a day or two before. She told a friend all about it, how it was for protection from a prowler. I know you get prowlers in that neighborhood, and there was a call just last night when somebody spotted a young fellow in a hooded sweatshirt on the next block. So he gave her this to let her feel at ease, and within a day or so she went and shot him with it.

"Shot him in the upper abdomen, had the gun pressed right into his flesh, so it left powder burns on his shirt and right through into the wound itself. What we think, he had her pressed up against this little computer table, and she tried fighting him off. She kept her nails short on account of she was some kind of a massage therapist and had a diploma to prove it, but they were long enough for her to get some of his skin under them and leave a few good scratches on his face. DNA'll confirm it, but you don't need lab results to know what you're looking at.

"Now a low-powered small-caliber slug two inches north of a man's navel is enough to get his attention, but it's not gonna pick him up and bounce him off the back wall. He didn't even bother to take the gun away from her, just went on squeezing her throat until he choked her out. Broke the hyoid bone, left those petechial hemorrhages on her eyes and damn well crushed that little gal's throat.

"So she's dead and he's been shot, and he leaves her lying there with the gun in her hand, and it looks as though he walked around a little, got his blood here and there. Pours himself a big glass of whiskey, or maybe he poured it earlier, but he doesn't drink it, because it was full to the brim when we found it.

"Now a glass of whiskey's not the best choice for something to pour into a stomach that's already got a bullet in it, but I don't know that he thought it through. If I was to guess it'd be that he poured the whiskey and then forgot about it for having other things on his mind.

"Like taking her framed massage diploma off the wall and smashing it, and picking things up and throwing them around. Which is the sort of thing a man might do in his situation, but then he did something I never heard of before. Wrote on the wall. *'God forgive me.'*

"I don't mean I never heard of anybody writing that or something like it. Man loses it, does something horrible, then has this moment where he realizes what he's done. Right about then, I'd have to say asking for forgiveness had to be a pretty natural response.

"What I never heard of before is *how* he did it. Took his finger and stuck it in the hole where she shot him and wrote the letters on the wall in his own blood. *'God forgive me.'* Well, you'd about have to, wouldn't you, if you was the Lord? Man goes to that kind of trouble to ask, you got to figure he means it.

"Then he may have been trying to go upstairs, but the staircase was as far as he got, because that's where we found him. Sitting on the third step, leaning back against the wall, one foot braced against the newel post. He had another gun, not the one he gave her. This was a revolver, a thirty-two, and he must have just picked it up because he doesn't seem to have gotten around to registering it. Maybe took it from one of his colored tenants against back rent. Wouldn't make him the first landlord to do so.

"Well, you get the picture. Barrel in his mouth, fingers wrapped around the butt, thumb on the trigger. *Blam!*

"All it took. Blew out the back of his head, left blood and brains on the wall behind him.

"Makes you wonder. Well, about no end of things, but one of them's the wife, Lisa. A woman looks to hire a pro to kill her husband, it's hard to work up a lot of sympathy for her. And George is an affluent businessman, important in his community, so you don't right off assume he was the kind of husband who had it coming.

"But spend a little time at the murder scene and your perspective shifts some. I wouldn't want to guess what he might have put that woman through over the course of a couple of years.

"Even so, there's things you have to do. I went over first thing in the morning and got the maid to wake her. Then I sat down with her and told her what had happened. She said she didn't know about any girlfriend, but you got the feeling that she might have had an inkling, and that this wouldn't have been the first young friend of George's to get a little help with the rent.

"Everything else shocked her, though. Murder and suicide, even if there's no love left in a marriage, that's not something to take in your stride. She came across as seriously shaken, and if she was faking it, Meryl Streep's got herself some serious competition.

"She was at the restaurant for her full shift. Not that there's a way on earth she could have barged in on the two of them and made that happen. Or hired it done. Hit men are professionals, whether they're Frankie from New Jersey or that guy they made the movie about. The Iceman? Something like that.

"Man's in that line of work, last thing he wants to do is get fancy. He makes the kill and goes home."

THIRTY-FOUR

For that day and the two days following, he never left the house. He spent hours at the computer, checking every site that might conceivably have news of the murder-suicide on Stapleton Terrace. There wasn't much news, and it was always the same.

And if there was a break in the case, he wouldn't learn about it on his computer. There'd be a knock on his door.

That's what he was waiting for, a knock on the door. A couple of cars outside, one from the Gallatin County Sheriff's Office, another from the state police.

Maybe a whole fleet of them. Men standing around looking grim, wearing vests, holding automatic rifles.

Or maybe it would just be Radburn, all by himself, with nothing but the holstered Colt he wore on his hip. Just stopping by with a couple of questions…

Because one thing was sure. He wasn't going to get away with it.

He was so sure of this that his behavior might have been designed to make it come true. Waiting for them, anticipating their arrival at any moment, he kept changing his mind about the nature of his eventual response.

At first he planned to meet them at the door, hands out in front of him, waiting for the cuffs. The words playing in his mind were variations on a theme, all of them admissions of guilt. *"I did it." "Okay you got me."* And, as the hours stretched, *"What took you so long?"*

At some point during the evening of the first day, he went to the closet and came back with the Smith & Wesson revolver. He made sure it was loaded and put it on the table to the right of his computer. His hand found the mouse and he checked a website; when he found nothing of interest, his hand moved of its own accord from the mouse to the gun butt.

He took the gun along when he stationed himself in front of the television set. He watched a local newscast, then turned to TCM, where they were showing *D.O.A.* He'd seen it several times over the years, with Edmund O'Brien unforgettable as the doomed poisoning victim who walks into the police station to report his own murder.

It matched his mood even if it didn't help it any, and as he watched he toyed with the gun like a monk with a string of worry beads.

When he went to bed he put the gun on the night table. He didn't expect to fall asleep, and the next thing he knew the room was bright with dawn. He bolted out of bed, reaching for the gun with one hand while the other groped for something to cover himself from the watching eyes.

But there were no eyes on him, no invaders in his house.

Nor was the gun where he'd left it, and that gave him another moment of panic until he located it under his pillow. Sometime during the night he'd evidently felt a need to have it closer.

He swung out the cylinder, confirmed that the weapon was still fully loaded. He closed the cylinder and put the gun under the pillow, then moved it to the night table. Neither place seemed right to him, and he carried the thing into the bathroom and set it on the edge of the sink while he showered.

And kept an eye on it while he shaved.

✿

When he moved to the computer, the gun went with him. When he split an English muffin and dropped it in the toaster, the gun was a few feet from his hand.

A little later, when he heard a car on Osprey Drive, he grabbed for the gun and held it with his finger on the trigger. The car pulled into his driveway, and he took a step toward his front door, determined to hold onto the gun but not yet sure what he was going to do with it.

The car backed out, headed off in the direction it had come from. People lost their way in the maze of creek-bound culs-de-sac, and now and then one of them used his driveway to turn around.

He walked to the door, opened it, looked around. Nothing, nobody.

Two hours later he remember the muffin and plucked it out of the toaster. It had reached just the right stage of doneness, but was cold and hard. He dropped it in the trash and left the room.

At the computer, he tried to compose a note. He opened a new document in Word and typed *I did it*.

Edmund O'Brien, after that long walk through the halls of the police station, had spun out a tale that lasted close to ninety minutes, clear to the end of the movie. And all he could seem to manage was three little words.

I did it. He looked at what he'd written and tried to think what else he could add. Tell them how he'd done it? How he'd waited for Ashley Hannon, how he'd moved in behind her when she entered the house, how he'd clapped a hand over her mouth and wrapped an arm to catch her neck in the crook of his elbow.

How she'd struggled against the choke hold. You weren't supposed to use it to subdue criminals, because now and then it worked a little too well, inducing a sleep from which the subject never awakened.

His was a good choke hold, easily maintained until her struggles ceased and she went limp in his arms. She was still breathing, and there was no visible bruising to her throat. That wouldn't show up until later, if at all, and there would be other bruises to eclipse it.

Should he write all that down?

He grew weary at the thought of it. The worst part of being a cop, he'd often thought, were the reports you had to write, and the most important consideration, as he'd learned early on, was CYA. The report could cover any number of topics, but what you really had to do was Cover Your Ass.

But how did you do that in a confession? When you led off with *I did it*, weren't you essentially *un*covering your ass? Wasn't that the point?

A little later he got the Ruger from the kitchen cupboard, loaded the magazine, and jacked a round into the chamber.

Doak "Two Guns" Miller, he thought.

He'd used an automatic and a revolver on Stapleton Terrace, and left them both there. Now he was sitting in his house with an automatic in one hand and a revolver in the other, and no clear idea what he wanted of them.

When they came for him, he could go out in a blaze of glory. Suicide by cop, they called it. You had a gun in your hand and you were firing at them, and the cops had no real choice in the matter. They fired back, and generally emptied their guns in the process, and even if they were lousy shots you were pretty much certain to wind up with a tag on your toe.

He looked down at his feet. He was wearing cargo shorts and a tee shirt, and his feet were bare, and he pictured his big toe with a tag on it.

Saying what? *Use No Hooks?*

Suicide by cop. In the movies, the bad guy would snarl his

intention to take as many cops with him as he could. That might make a kind of emotional sense if you hated cops, but Bill Radburn was the closest thing he had to a friend in the whole state of Florida, so why would he want to kill him? Or anyone else who might come through the door?

I did it.

Yeah, no shit, Sherlock. Like you're telling them what they don't already know.

After he'd choked her unconscious, after he'd moved her to where he wanted her, there was a question of timing. Ideally, he'd hold off on the next step until just before Otterbein's arrival, but you couldn't set your clock by the man, could you?

Say he waited until he saw the Lincoln's lights in the driveway. The choke hold wouldn't keep her out forever. And how long would it take Otterbein to make his way from behind the wheel to inside the house?

He waited as long as he dared. Then he heard her breathing change, and the next thing would be her eyes opening, and he couldn't let that happen. If he had to look into her eyes—

No.

He got his hands around her throat, and every image came flooding in at him. Phyllis, that dizzy bitch: *"Choke me, will you? Come on, how tricky is that?"* And Roberta, with his hands on her throat, hands that wanted so desperately to tighten, until he willed them to move from throat to abdomen.

And the story he'd told to Barb Hamill, with the girl a combination of both women, an unmarried and pregnant version who liked to be choked but got more than she bargained for: *"And what I do, I just keep squeezing. Both hands, as tight as I can make them, and she starts twitching like a fish on a line…"*

Yeah, pretty much like that.

*

I did it.

Only one reason to write it down, whether it was three words or every detail he could remember. All it could be, long or short, was a suicide note.

Suicide by cop?

He didn't need to wait for a cop to turn up. He was a cop himself, wasn't he?

Had been, anyway.

Now he was a murderer.

Two-Gun Miller, with a revolver in one hand and an automatic in the other. If he waited for them, the best he could hope for was to go down shooting. If he surrendered, if they captured him alive, the death sentence was a foregone conclusion. He'd killed two people in a particularly vicious fashion, and it would be hard for any lawyer with a straight face to argue mitigating circumstances.

And why fight the death sentence? Whatever cocktail of drugs they fed into your veins, it had to be better than life without parole. And can we skip the appeals? Florida was pretty good at killing people, and he'd make it as easy for them as he could.

Still, it wasn't the Old West, they didn't find you guilty on Tuesday for what you did on Monday, then drop a rope around your neck first thing Wednesday morning. Even if he greased the skids, he was looking at a year or more in a cell.

Wouldn't welcome that.

THIRTY-FIVE

He went to the bathroom, came back, sat down, picked up a gun in each hand. Took turns trying them in different positions. In his mouth, angled up and back, poised to send a bullet through the palate and into the brain—and, as with George Otterbein, out through the back of the skull. Pressed into his belly just below the solar plexus—much easier now, with his own hand and his own stomach, than when he'd propped up Otterbein's unconscious body and wrapped his own hand around Ashley's limp hand and helped her dead finger squeeze the trigger.

That wound hadn't been enough to kill George, that's not what it was for, and it had taken another blow to the back of the head to keep the man unconscious. Then he'd manhandled him over to the staircase, stuck George's index finger in the abdominal wound and wiped it imperfectly.

He unloaded the Taurus, reloaded it with George's fingerprints on the shells. Got his prints on the gun butt as well, including one from the bloody index finger. Then he'd used his own finger to force George's thumb on the trigger.

And he'd dipped his own finger into the belly wound so that he could inscribe George's confession on the wall. He remembered that famous case, some loony leaving messages on a mirror, *Stop me before I kill more*, but that hardly applied, and in the end he'd settled for *God forgive me*.

Fat chance.

George's blood, but his own finger. So who then was the one seeking divine forgiveness?

Consciously, he'd been doing nothing more or less than staging a scene. But on another level…

He clamped his eyes shut, blinked the thought away. Both guns now, one in the belly and one in the mouth, and could he summon the nerve to work both triggers at the same time?

And what would Radburn and his merry men make of that?

No appetite.

At one point he went to the kitchen. There was a single English muffin left, and he split it and toasted it. Buttered it, took a bite, and the process of chewing and swallowing seemed too much of a chore, and pointless in the bargain.

Tossed it. Watched some TV.

Half an hour into the movie, he had a look at the computer. The screen had gone dark, but he touched a key and saw the open Word document.

I did it.

Nothing to add, nothing to subtract. He watched the rest of the movie and went to bed.

The third day was more of the same. He didn't even try to eat, just sipped some water when he was aware of thirst.

Late in the day he went out of the house for the first time, but only to walk out onto the dock. He stood there looking out at nothing, then went back inside.

Went to bed again, woke up again.

And everything was different.

THIRTY-SIX

He got up, showered, shaved. He went to the computer and backspaced through *I did it*, erasing the words. His version of Word automatically backed up every document, but not until after you'd saved it once. He checked anyway, and while he was at it he cleared the browser's history for the past week.

They weren't coming for him. It had taken days for him to entertain the thought, but he'd somehow awakened at last with it all clear in his mind. His efforts on Stapleton Terrace, his over-elaborate staging of the scene, had actually worked to make two deaths go in the books as a murder and suicide. George Otterbein had killed his much younger paramour, Ashley Hannon, sustaining a profound but non-fatal wound in the process. And then, overcome with remorse, he'd taken his own life.

Case closed.

His every action at the murder scene had been undertaken with great care and foresight, keeping him too busy getting it right to let other thoughts intrude. And yet all along he'd carried the unvoiced conviction that he was doomed, that his role would be instantly apparent, that they'd come for him before the bodies were cold.

And so he'd arrived home and promptly fallen apart. From the moment he cleared his own threshold he was waiting to be arrested, and all evidence to the contrary, starting with Sheriff Radburn's words on the phone, failed to change his mind.

He'd be caught, he knew it. Forensics would find his skin cells mixed with Otterbein's blood on the wall. A neighbor who'd helpfully written down his plate number would call it in. Someone who'd caught a glimpse of him would remember an older and whiter face than you usually saw framed by a hoodie, and would pick his picture out of the six-pack they showed him.

The mood that came down on him was paralyzing, and all he'd been able to do was outlast it—and, with a little more pressure on the two triggers, he wouldn't have done so. But he was alive, and in his right mind, or as close to it as he could reasonably expect to get.

And now he had work to do.

The clothes he'd bought at J. C. Penney and worn to Stapleton Terrace, the black pants and hoodie and sneakers, were on the floor of his closet, stuffed into the shopping bag they'd come in. There was blood on them, and gunshot residue, and all manner of DNA—his, of course, and that of his victims as well.

Just sitting on his closet floor, waiting for someone to find them.

He carried the bag to his car and headed for the dump, stopping along the way for a bag of charcoal and a pint can of lighter fluid. The clerk who took his cash and rang him up volunteered that her husband had bought them a propane grill, and she'd never go back to charcoal.

"Well, y'all are modern," he said. "Myself, I'm too darn old to change."

There were piles of smoldering trash at the dump. He dumped the bag of clothes on one of them, and tongues of flame greeted the fresh offering. He added squirts of lighter fluid and watched everything burn.

Opened the sack of charcoal, emptied it in another part of the dump. Wiped the can and tossed it. Brought back the empty sack, added it to the fire.

Driving back, he thought, Jesus, they had their chance. Three days in his closet, a bagful of hanging evidence, right there for anybody to see.

And nobody did. So fuck 'em.

His stomach had been trying to get his attention all morning, and on his way back from the dump he was able to pay attention and grasp the nature of its complaint. He hadn't really eaten in days.

He filled a shopping cart at the Winn-Dixie. When he got home he put everything away, looked over his purchases, and went out to Denny's. He ordered the Hungry Man's Breakfast and ate everything they put in front of him. Eggs, bacon, sausage, ham, pancakes, hash browns—a mountain of food, and he cleaned his plate.

Back home, he turned the radio to a local station and let it play while he sat at the computer, checking news accounts.

Nothing, not really. Some of the national media had picked up the story, and if they'd gotten anything juicy they might have run with it. If, say, a B-list star had hopped onto her massage table back in Clearwater, or if she'd at least been arrested a couple of times. But she hadn't, and the man who killed her was a fairly colorless local businessman who'd never done anything newsworthy until the last day of his life. So they'd covered the story in a paragraph and let it die.

Nothing.

He stepped away from the computer, turned off the radio, sat down on the couch.

And, for the first time in days, he let himself think about Lisa.

There'd been no point, really, in giving her space in his head for the past several days. He couldn't call her. His phone was gone, smashed and trashed before he'd paid his last visit to the duplex.

He thought about her now.

Thought about his first sight of her, on Radburn's phone. And then on his own phone, after the sheriff had emailed the picture to him.

Had he ever deleted it?

He reached for his phone, opened up Camera Roll. There she was, and he sat for a moment looking at her picture and remembering. Remembering the first real physical glimpse of her, at the Cattle Baron. And then in his car, watching all the changes of expression on her face and in her eyes as she came to realize what was going on.

Other places, other times.

He thought about the fantasy, and how it had begun to fade as soon as he'd brought it fully into focus. There she was, Fantasy Girl, all he'd ever envisioned and more, and all they had to do was get in the car, his car or her car, and point it away from Gallatin County, and drive.

Not a chance.

So another fantasy had taken its place, this one to grow out of a simple act of murder. It had been a sufficiently powerful dream to make killers out of John Garfield and Fred MacMurray.

And look how well it had worked out for those two.

He went back to the computer, found what he was looking for. Picked up his phone, made a call, talked for a few minutes.

Rang off.

The 4PM feature on TCM was *The Last Seduction*, a 1994 film starring Linda Fiorentino. He'd never seen her before, not that he remembered, and he didn't see how he could have forgotten her.

If you were going to cast Fantasy Girl, well, she'd sail through the auditions.

It was a terrific movie, classic film noir given a more con-
temporary slant, and Fiorentino was almost too convincing in
the role of a homicidal sociopath who uses her sexual skills to
turn men into killers. At the end she tricks one of them into
confessing to a murder she herself committed, and winds up in
the clear with all of the cash.

He watched the entire credit roll before he turned it off.
Not the best picture to be watching, he thought, given his present circumstances.

Maybe it was a sign to call that number again: *"Listen, I
changed my mind since I spoke to you two hours ago. I'm going
to cancel."*

No, he thought. The cards were dealt. Play the hand.

It was just past 7:30 when he pulled into the lot at the Cattle
Baron. He didn't see her car, and wondered if she'd returned to
work yet. She might have felt it necessary to spend a little more
time playing the grieving widow, might simply want to give the
scandal a few more days to die down before making herself
available to the public.

Or she might have quit the job. She certainly didn't need it,
neither for the money it paid nor for the excuse it provided to
get out of the house. She was a rich widow, she lived by herself,
and she could do as she pleased and go where she wanted.

He took another turn through the lot, looking for a Lincoln
this time. They'd have returned George's car to Rumsey Road,
after forensics had found nothing in it but whatever prints and
trace evidence George had left there, and maybe she'd want a
change from the Lexus.

But no, there was the Lexus, parked where she always parked
it, in the very spot where she'd left it unlocked, with the Baby
Browning waiting for him beneath the front seat.

How had he missed it the first time? Maybe it was a message

from his guardian angel, the same one who'd tried to use Linda Fiorentino to get him to change his mind and cancel. Maybe—

He parked the Chevy and went into the restaurant.

She was seating a party of six when he reached the hostess stand. He watched her moving smoothly among them, making small talk, smiling. Then she straightened up, steered a waitress to their table, and headed back to her post. She had almost reached it when she registered who was waiting for her.

And if he hadn't been looking at her face, watching her eyes, he might have missed her reaction. It didn't show in her body language, only on her face. He fancied he could see her thoughts written on her forehead, and they all ended with question marks.

But when she was within a few feet of him she flashed her hostess smile and asked him if he'd be dining alone. Or would someone be joining him?

"I'm by myself," he said.

"Right this way," she said, smoothly, professionally, and led him to a table off to the left. It was set for two, and she scooped up the napkin and silverware opposite him. As she straightened up, the tip of one finger traced a two-inch line across the back of his hand.

No one watching could have seen a thing.

"Your waitress will be right with you," she said, and walked out of his field of vision.

He chose the same meal he'd had last time, unable to think of any way to improve on it, and ordered it from the same dishwater blonde. He remembered her name—Cindy—but she didn't recognize him until he specified that he wanted his steak cooked black and blue. Her eyes widened at the phrase, and she looked at him and said, "Oh, hi! It's been a while, hasn't it?"

He said he'd been busy.

The rib eye was just right, as were the baked potato and creamed spinach, and he ate with good appetite. He'd stuffed himself earlier at Denny's, but that had been a good many hours ago, and the several days without food had given him some catching up to do.

He drank a bottle of Dutch beer with his meal, and rounded it off with a piece of chess pie and two cups of coffee. When he saw Lisa on her way over, he got out the index card on which he'd printed a few words in large block caps.

She asked if he'd enjoyed his meal. Very much, he said, and positioned the card so she could read it.

She dropped her voice and said, "Tomorrow?"

"Around noon, if that works."

"I can make it work."

Her hand settled on his, just for a moment, and he looked up and met her eyes.

So blue…

Cindy brought the check. He paid cash, left a decent tip. Outside, he stood alongside his car for a moment and watched a cloud move to cover the moon.

He got in the car, headed for home thinking about blue eyes.

Thought about the movie.

Linda Fiorentino's eyes, he'd noticed, were green.

Well, there you go, he told himself. All the difference in the world.

Before he went to bed, he sat at the kitchen table with both his guns, the .38 registered to him and the 9mm from the show in Quitman. He'd never fired either one of them, but all the same he gave them both a thorough cleaning.

Loaded them when he was done, and put them away.

THIRTY-SEVEN

At the Chiefland Mall the next day, she apologized for keeping him waiting. "My lawyer came over," she said, "with a stack of papers for me to sign, and it took forever. I'd have called you, but—"

"I wasn't waiting that long," he said. "And I had the car radio to keep me company. Waylon Jennings, Dottie West, and your pal Emmy Lou."

"Country Gold. Close your eyes and you'd think you were back at Kimberley's Kove."

"Or half a mile away at Tourist Court."

"No music, though."

"Sure there was," he said. "We made our own."

Her Lexus was parked alongside his Monte Carlo, and they stood a foot apart between the two vehicles.

She said, "Well, shall we head over to the love nest? I guess you must have paid them for another two weeks."

He shook his head. "I let it run out. That's no place for us now, with the musty carpet and the drapes smelling of smoke. I booked us into an oceanfront condo a few miles down the road. It's somebody's unsalable time share and they're more than happy to rent it by the day."

"It sounds very nice."

"I haven't seen it yet. I found it online and booked it over the phone. No, let's leave my car and take yours."

The one-bedroom apartment was on the seventh floor of a ten-story building. It had a balcony with an ocean view. The floor was black and white ceramic tile, set in a geometric pattern, with a brace of area rugs in bright primary colors.

The bed was queen size, the bed linen gleaming white.

Lisa walked through the place, getting the feel of it, making it hers. "Quite a step up," she said. "It doesn't feel *Back Street* at all, does it? I kind of liked that aspect of the places we've been before, but you're right, this is better for us now." She'd been looking out a window, and turned to face him. "I'm scared to death," she said.

"So am I."

"I can't even think, let alone make whole sentences. I wish I was in the mood. Are you?"

"In the mood?"

"You're not. We're neither of us horny, are we? Doak?" He looked at her. "Fuck me anyway. Okay?"

"Oh, God," she said. "I was so scared."

"That it wouldn't work."

"That it wouldn't work, that we'd used it all up. That you'd look at me and see ugly where you used to see beautiful."

"That couldn't happen."

"But how could I know that? I was half an hour late today. More than that, closer to forty minutes. You must have been wondering if you were going to get stood up."

"It crossed my mind."

"Mine too. The last time we talked, you told me how to disable my phone and get rid of it. I didn't want to, it was like cutting a lifeline, but I did what you said. I think I told you I was keeping one message of yours."

"Yes."

"And you said to delete it, and I did. And after I did it I had the thought that I would probably never hear your voice again."

He waited.

"And I went to work, and I wondered what was going to happen, and when it was going to happen. And I told myself it wouldn't be for a few days, if it ever happened at all. And I didn't know what I wanted, I really didn't. So I worked my hours, and I smiled and talked nice to people and did my job the way I always did my job.

"And I went home, half expecting him to be there when I walked in the house. But he wasn't there and his car was gone, and there were no phone messages, and I took a soak in the tub and kept waiting for the phone to ring, but it didn't.

"And then the maid woke me to tell me the Sheriff was waiting downstairs in the front hall. But that was all she could tell me, because he hadn't said anything to her. And I got dressed, and I made sure I was wearing something comfortable in case I was going to wind up wearing it in jail."

"Jesus."

"Well, I didn't know what was going on. But I had to go downstairs, and I did, and I got the girl to bring us coffee in the living room, and he told me he had some bad news, and I learned that George murdered a young woman in her apartment, that she shot him while he was strangling her but it didn't keep him from finishing the job, and that then he went nuts and wrote his confession on the wall. And went and shot himself, and now he was dead."

She frowned. "And I was waiting for the rest of it, you know? Waiting for the questions, waiting for him to spring the trap. But he didn't, he was all sympathy and consideration, and did I want a doctor? Did I want someone to give me a sedative?

"And he went away, finally, and then it all went on playing out, with his kids and everybody's lawyers and a woman from the local weekly who thinks she's Brenda Fucking Starr, and throughout the next couple of days I just acted numb and dazed and brain-dead, and it wasn't an act.

"And all the time, where is Doak? Where the fuck is Doak?"

"I couldn't—"

"Oh, I know that. I knew it then. The one thing you couldn't possibly do was get in touch with me." She put a hand on his chest. "But then something strange happened. You disappeared."

"I disappeared?"

"Uh-huh. From the county, the state. You didn't live here anymore. You just drove away. That's what I decided must have happened."

"After the—"

"After it happened. But then that shifted, too."

"How?"

"You spoke to me, and you told me to get rid of my phone. And then you got in your car and disappeared."

"I never went to Stapleton Terrace."

"That's right."

"And what happened there—"

"Happened the way Sheriff Radburn said. They had a fight, he started choking her, she shot him, he finished killing her, he realized what he'd done, and—"

"And so on."

"Right. And so on."

He thought about it. "The little gun, the Browning with the malachite grips. You left it in your car for me. How'd Ashley wind up with it?"

"You gave it to her, told her he might get violent and she might need it for protection. Or you just slipped into the house and left it where she could find it."

"All loaded and ready for use."

"I guess."

He let it play through his mind. "Well, it could have happened that way. And I can see how it would be emotionally convenient if it did."

"Because it's nobody's fault. Except George's, and he paid for it."

" 'God forgive me.' "

"Huh?"

"On the wall."

"Oh, yes, of course. For a moment I thought you were—"

"Praying?"

She looked off into the middle distance. "I was alone," she said, "and he was dead, and it wasn't my fault."

"And I was out of the picture."

"And you were out of the picture, so I didn't let myself think about you, because what was the point? There was this man I used to know, and for a little while we loved each other, and then he went away."

"You didn't really think it."

"That you had run off? I don't know what I thought or what I made myself think. I didn't expect you last night. I must have looked stunned."

"Well, I could tell you were surprised. But you didn't show much."

"The perfect hostess," she said. "Poised and unflappable. 'You'll be dining alone this evening? Right this way, sir.'"

"I didn't know how I'd feel, seeing you."

"I didn't know how I *felt*. And then to have to meet you at the mall. How could I do that? I'm so glad you found this place. If we'd had to go back to that room—"

"No, that was never an option."

"Although we had some moments there, didn't we? Telling each other stories. Did you bring me any stories today? No?"

He drew a breath. "After the incident—"

"That's a good word for it."

"Afterward, I never left the house until yesterday. I watched old movies and waited for them to arrest me."

"You thought that would happen?"

"I knew it would. I sat there with a gun in each hand waiting for a knock on the door."

"Somewhere," she said, "there's a Jehovah's Witness with no idea what he missed. Until yesterday, you said. What changed your mind?"

"Time."

"The great healer. And until then it was just you and some old movies. No juicy phone calls from Real Estate Girl?"

"That's over."

"Really?"

"Really. I spoke to her earlier and managed to scare her off."

"I won't ask how. And Pregnant Girl? But you don't want to talk about Pregnant Girl, do you?"

"Not now."

"Okay."

"What I should do now," he said, "is tell you what happened that night."

"I guess it didn't just happen by itself."

"No."

"Darling, we can just—"

"Skip it?"

"Oh, I guess we can't, can we? Lie close to me, and let's pull the covers up over us. And could you do what you did once before? Could you put your finger inside me while you tell me? I don't know why that should make me feel safer, I really don't. But it does."

THIRTY-EIGHT

He told it straight through, from his arrival at the house on Stapleton Terrace to his return to Osprey Drive. His voice was level and unemotional throughout, his narrative limited to a recital of uninflected facts. *I did this and I did that and I did this and I did that…*

She heard him all the way through without interruption. When he was done she lay still and remained silent. Their bodies were almost touching, and the blanket covered them like a cocoon.

Her eyes were closed, her breathing deep and even. Softly, he said, "Lisa?"

"I'm awake."

"I wasn't sure."

"I was there with you just now, you know. Standing at your shoulder watching it all happen. How awful it must have been for you."

"I think we can safely say it was worse for them."

"But then it was over, wasn't it? For them, but not for you." She reached to touch his face. "What shocked me, when he came and told me—"

"The girl."

"It never once occurred to me that she would be part of it."

"There was no way to leave her out," he said. "Not that I could think of. If George gets killed, even if he drives into a creek or gets sucked into a sinkhole, they've got to come looking for you. The only way I could think of that would work was for him to kill himself, and to stage that and make it look right, you had to have another person on the scene. And she had to be the kind of witness who couldn't contradict you."

"Because she was dead."

"And her death made his suicide plausible. It gave him a reason. I don't know, maybe there was another way to handle it. But this was the only one I could come up with."

"And it worked. No, don't take your hand away, I want your fingers in me. Unless your hand is bothering you."

"No."

"You could move your fingers if you wanted. Just a little, so they don't cramp up on you. Oh, that's just so nice. Darling? When you told me about the man in New York, the one you had to shoot."

"Yes."

"You told me how it felt."

"This was different," he said.

"It wasn't thrilling."

"No." He took a moment to review the memory. "There was no feeling attached to any of it," he said. "A little revulsion, I suppose, but it was off to the side and out of the way. I was aware of it after the fact, but I didn't have time to pay any attention to it while it was going on. I had these things I had to do and I was doing them."

"Checking them off the list."

"Sort of. Working hard to get them done right."

He took a breath. *You don't have to say this*, he told himself. Took another breath. *Yes, you do.*

He said, "Before I went over there, I ran it through my imagination."

"Like a visualization exercise."

"I suppose so. And I thought it would be exciting. I got hard at the thought of taking hold of her, and doing her."

"Strangling her."

"Strangling her. And then it was as I described it. Passionless, robotic. That's while it was going on. Afterward it was—"

"Awful."

"Worse than awful."

"It's over now, baby."

"I know."

"You can let go of it. That's what we're doing, we're letting go of it."

He nodded. "But first," he said, "I have to tell you about Roberta Ellison."

"I don't know who that is. Oh, wait! Pregnant Girl? Don't tell me you went back to see her after all? You did! Oh, I want to hear this. Did you get to fuck her?"

He told her the stratagem he'd used, making sure the little boy had gone up for his nap. Told her how he'd noticed perfume on his return, known the opportunity was there for him. Told her how he'd shocked the woman (*"Do you suppose he eats her pussy?"*) and manipulated her until she led him upstairs.

He lay beside her, facing her, breathing her breath, sharing her body heat beneath the blanket, keeping his fingers tucked snugly inside her. The earlier narrative had been dry and clinical, but he recounted this episode as it had happened, and as he talked she began moving against his hand, moving around his fingers, making little sounds deep in her throat.

When she'd caught her breath she said, "Oh, baby, if she had half as good a time as I did just now, she's got to be the happiest Milf around."

"I left something out," he said.

"That's okay, darling. That's a super bedtime story and I won't mind hearing it again the next time you tell it to me. And just think of all the bedtime stories you'll get to tell me. Years and years of stories."

"Think so?"

She propped herself up on an elbow. "Oh, I do," she said. "Isn't that what you want? For us to be together?"

"Of course."

"I'm still Fantasy Girl, right?"

"Right."

"Because otherwise what's the fucking point? You know?"

"I know."

"We got away with it, and I'm a rich widow. And for a while I've got to go on being a rich widow living on Rumsey Road, and you've got to be an ex-cop on Osprey Drive. But there'll come a time when it's okay for us to meet."

"We already met."

"At the Baron? Oh, when I thought you were a hit man. Who knows about that? Just Bill Radburn? Okay, so in a couple of weeks you come to the Baron again, and we'll flirt a little. And the next day you have a beer with the sheriff and tell him you saw me at the Baron and I didn't even recognize you from the Winn-Dixie lot, and we sort of hit it off, and you were thinking of asking me out. And you're a little hesitant, and what does he think, and he tells you to go for it."

"And we start seeing each other."

"And it's a perfectly dignified courtship, because they don't have to see the part where we're fucking each other's brains out in a rented time share somewhere."

"And we get married," he said.

"When the time's right. If you think you'd want to be married to me. If I'm still Fantasy Girl."

"You'll always be Fantasy Girl."

"Then I don't see a problem. I don't want to live in that fucking house of his. I'm glad I get to own it, but I'll be way happier when I get to sell it. If we stay in the area I'd just as soon keep my job, but we don't have to. We could live anywhere. Do you care where we live?"

"No."

"Neither do I. I'm not rich-rich, but I'll always have some money, and you've got your pension—"

"Whoopee."

"No, really. We've got enough to be comfortable, and that's plenty." She stopped, looked at him. "I'm chattering away, all excited, and you're not. Is something wrong?"

"I have to tell you the rest of the story," he said.

And he told her how his hands had found Pregnant Girl's pale throat, and how his excitement had built with the urge to apply pressure.

"I wanted to kill her," he said. "I don't know how close I came. How do you measure that sort of distance? I know my hands were ready, they wanted so much to tighten their grip that it was almost impossible to hold them back."

"And then what happened?"

"I let go of her throat."

"Where did you put your hands?"

"On her stomach."

"And the urge you'd felt—"

"Passed."

"And now you can't stop thinking about it."

"That's right."

"And you had to tell me so I'll know to be afraid of you."

"Something like that."

"Give me a minute, let me think. Okay. Put your hands on my neck."

"The hell I will."

"The hell you *won't*. I'm serious, baby. Okay, you're on your side, and I'm going to lie facing away from you, and I want you to put your hands on my throat. God damn it, Doak, just do it, will you please? Now how do you feel?"

"Sick to my stomach."

"Are you excited?"

"I just told you, I'm—"

"Sick to your stomach. Do you want to wring my neck?"

"Jesus, Lisa—"

"Because you can, you know. You're bigger and stronger and I'm not even struggling, I'm just lying here. Is it exciting that I'm helpless?"

"No."

"You can move your hands now. Do what you did with her, hold my stomach. It doesn't pooch out and you're not likely to feel anything kicking, but hold me anyway. Baby, I'm not afraid of you. You're not gonna kill me."

And later she said, "I'm glad you insisted on telling me the rest of the story. And I'm glad I made you put your hands on my throat. It's good to have all of that out of the way. Everything's gonna work out for us, you know."

"I'm beginning to believe it."

"But we still have some big issues to deal with. Like, do you think I should let my hair grow long again?"

"I like it like this."

"So do I. See? Some big issues, and we just settled one of them. Everything's working out."

He was silent, thinking it through. At length he said, "You know, in the movies I've been watching, things never work out. In the end, something always goes wrong."

"That's the movies," she said. "This is life."

Don't Let the Mystery End Here.
Try These Other Great Books From
HARD CASE CRIME!

Hard Case Crime brings you gripping, award-winning crime fiction
by best-selling authors and the hottest new writers in the field.
Find out what you've been missing:

Grifter's Game
by LAWRENCE BLOCK

Con man Joe Marlin was used to scoring easy cash off beautiful
women. But that was before he met Mona Brassard and found
himself facing the most dangerous con of his career, one that
will leave him either a killer—*or a corpse.*

RAVES FOR THE WORK OF
LAWRENCE BLOCK

"Block grabs you…and never lets go."
— Elmore Leonard

"The reader is riveted to the words, the action."
— Robert Ludlum

*"Marvelous…will hold readers
gaga with suspense."*
— New York Newsday

*"He is simply the best at what he does…
If you haven't read him before, you've
wasted a lot of time. Begin now."*
— Mostly Murder

**Available now at your favorite bookstore.
For more information, visit
www.HardCaseCrime.com**

Sexy Suspense From
An MWA Grand Master!

GETTING OFF
A Novel of Sex and Violence

by LAWRENCE BLOCK
WRITING AS JILL EMERSON

So this girl walks into a bar. When she walks out, there's a man with her. She goes to bed with him, and she likes that part. Then she kills him, and she likes that even better.

She's been doing this for a while, and she's good at it.

Then a chance remark gets her thinking of the men who got away, the lucky ones who survived a night with her.

And now she's a girl with a mission. Picking up their trails. Hunting them down. *Crossing them off her list…*

RAVES FOR THE WORK OF LAWRENCE BLOCK

"Sometimes you open up a book and you just know: You're in the hands of a master."
— Washington Post

"Addictive."
— Entertainment Weekly

"Reads like it's been jolted by factory-fresh defibrillator pads."
— Time

"Block grabs you…and never lets go."
— Elmore Leonard

**Available now at your favorite bookstore.
For more information, visit
www.HardCaseCrime.com**